MIDNIGHT POISON

ZARKOV BRATVA DUET
BOOK 2

PENNY DEE

Copyright © 2024 by Penny Dee

All rights reserved.

No part of this book may be reproduced in any form or by any electronic or mechanical means, including information storage and retrieval systems, without written permission from the author, except for the use of brief quotations in a book review.

This book is a work of fiction. Any references to real events, real people, and real places are used fictitiously. Other names, characters, places, and incidents are products of the author's imagination and any resemblance to persons, living or dead, actual events, organizations or places is entirely coincidental.

Disclaimer: The material in this book contains graphic language and sexual content and is intended for mature audiences ages 18 and older. **Please read Author's Note for content warnings.**

Developmental Editing by Sara-Jane Higgins (Kat's Literary Services)

Editing by Steph White (Kat's Literary Services)

Cover by Cormar Covers

For Rachael

AUTHOR'S NOTE

Thank you for choosing to read the Zarkov Bratva duet. This book continues on from book one, **Bratva Lullaby**, so you will need to read that before continuing with this book.

Because this duet is a mafia romance it includes some darker themes throughout the story, including kidnapping, assault, and murder. There is also a lot of sexual acts and profanity. But the real focus in this enemies-to-lovers romance is how love can conquer all and go on to thrive in a mafia world made for bloodshed. I hope you enjoy it.

DESCRIPTION

He took me as collateral to ensure my ex-fiancé kept the deal they made.

But since then, Lev Zarkov has become so much more than the devil I thought he was.

And now his baby is growing in my belly.

I don't want to leave him, but after one devastating night blows up our life, I know I have my baby to think about.

I tell myself that leaving is the right thing to do. But waking up without Lev in the middle of the night is pure midnight poison.

I miss his touch. His smell. The warm, comforting way he would hold me in his arms and let me know how much he wanted me.

But that isn't the man who comes after me.

He's angry. He's formidable. He's hurt.

And now that he's found me, he's going to make me pay for breaking his heart.

But there is a danger lurking in the shadows.

And we'll have to put our differences aside long enough to fight the invisible threat that could destroy everything.

Midnight Poison is book two in the Zarkov Bratva duet and concludes Brooke & Lev's story.

1

BROOKE

The explosion lights up the night, and the glass in the windows shakes. Outside, the night is lit up by a sudden orange glow before it's swallowed into the darkness.

Oh God, no...

Standing at the window, all I see is carnage in the parking lot below.

What used to be Lev's car is a smoldering wreck. It's a blackened shell of twisted metal. Glass is everywhere. Several feet away from the vehicle is what looks like a body.

No, please don't let it be Lev.

Then I realize it must be Igor, and my heart drops. Tears well in my eyes as I search for Lev.

Then I see him. He wasn't near the car, but the force of the blast sent him flying backward into the garden lining the sidewalk.

He's not moving.

He's dead.

The dread erupts in my chest, and I feel my knees go weak.

But then he moves, and a wave of relief washes over me.

I start banging on the window. I feel so helpless. I see a dark hooded figure walking toward him, its arm outstretched and pointing a gun at Lev. I scream and bang louder on the glass. I see Lev look up at me.

Don't look at me.

There's someone coming for you.

But the figure quickly diverts his path when two of Lev's men appear out of nowhere, followed by a swarm of hospital and security staff running outside to see what happened. I watch the dark figure turn away and disappear quickly into the darkness.

I don't bother with clothes or shoes or anything sensible like that. Instead, I try to flee the room, but one of the two men Lev has posted outside of my door tries to stop me.

"Get out of my way," I demand, desperate to get to Lev.

"The pakhan said—"

"The pakhan is lying out there injured."

"We heard the noise. Vinnie has gone to investigate. But you must stay here where it's safe."

I shove him in the chest. "Go help your pakhan. He needs you."

"The pakhan won't be happy if I leave you. Or let you leave this room."

I grab his collar. "You listen to me. Go and help your pakhan, or so help me God, I will shoot you myself."

He looks a little unsure. The noise drifting up from the parking lot is getting louder as more and more people join the commotion outside.

"We are to stay here," he says again.

"What is your name?" I ask.

He looks confused.

"It's not rocket science. I'm just asking for your name."

He frowns like he's never been asked the question before, then cautiously adds, "Toby."

I steady my breath and in a controlled voice say, "Right, Toby, I am going to leave this room with or without your help. What's it going to be?"

But he won't budge. "We stay."

The eerie wail of approaching police sirens cuts into the night.

I have to get to Lev.

Catching Toby off guard, I slam my elbow into his solar plexus and make a run for it. But with every step I take, my body protests. Every bruise lights up with pain as I make my way through the maze of corridors and stairwells to get outside.

By the time I burst outside, the night air is heavy with the stench of burning metal, and my body is screaming for me to stop. But I can't. I need to get to Lev. I need to know he is okay.

An EMT is with him, checking his vitals. Lev's eyes are closed. And suddenly, I'm terrified for him. My hand goes to my belly where our baby is nestled inside me.

I look around us. Everywhere is chaos. People yelling. Hospital staff running around. Bystanders appearing out of nowhere. I glance around at the people who have gathered to watch from a safe distance and scan the area for a figure in a hoodie. Is he here watching this unfold? Waiting for the right moment to finish what he started?

I shiver with dread. This was an assassination attempt.

"Miss, you shouldn't be out here," an EMT tells me as he rushes past. "There's glass and debris everywhere."

Toby appears by my side and he looks pissed. "You need to get back inside. There could be a secondary device."

More panic rolls through me. And suddenly, I'm being pulled away and ushered inside by Toby and another man who is yelling something, but I can't hear because all I can see is Lev being treated by the EMT on the ground.

And he doesn't look unconscious.

He looks dead.

2

BROOKE

"I need to see him," I yell at Toby and the other guard.

"Not yet, you don't. You need to stay inside with me and Vinnie," Toby says.

We're walking down a long corridor lit with florescent light.

"We're taking you back to your room," Vinnie adds. "And you'll stay there until we receive further information."

I try to yank myself free from Toby's grasp, but it's no use. His grip is strong and vice-like as he leads me down the corridor, further and further away from Lev.

A heavy wave of emotion surges through me when I think of him lying out there, broken and possibly dead, and I can't hide my panic and fear.

"Please, I can't leave him out there alone. He needs me. He's my—" I stop when I realize I don't even know what Lev is to me. He's no longer the man who took me from one life and forced me into another. *He's... he's...* "That's the father of my baby out there, please. We only just found out about the baby. I need to be with him."

A flicker of empathy crosses Vinnie's tough features. "Then you need to think about you and your baby, and not what is happening out there. That baby needs you to keep you both safe."

He's right.

It's not just me I have to think about anymore.

I can't go tearing into the blown-up evening without thought for my own safety. I've got precious cargo onboard.

But surely I'm safe inside the hospital.

Then I remember the hooded figure.

He's still at large.

Am I in danger?

Will he come after me and... oh my God, my baby?

The door at the end of the corridor bursts open, and an orderly hurries toward us, pushing a gurney. But as he nears us, he shoves the gurney toward Vinnie, knocking him to the ground. Realizing the threat, Toby releases me and reaches for his gun, but it's too late. The orderly shoots him between the eyes, then steps over his body and shoots Vinnie.

I scream, but the gunman hooks me around the neck with his arm and yanks me to his chest.

"When you weren't in your room, I thought I was going to have to go home empty-handed." His voice is deep and thick, with a heavy Russian accent. "But lucky me, here you are."

Fear blasts through me. *He went looking for me to...*

...to kill me?

With my back to his chest, I struggle against his grip. "Please, don't hurt me. I'm... I'm pregnant."

He tightens his hold on me.

"The pakhan has already produced an heir?" He chuckles. "Of course he has. If I had a sweet little whore like you, I wouldn't come up for air until she was full with my baby, either."

He drags his free hand down my body.

"It's such a shame that I'm short on time. I think I would like to sample me some of the pakhan's whore. Ruin that sweet pussy while it's still warm."

I twist my body away from his offending touch. "Please, think of my baby."

"Can't say I've fucked a pregnant whore before." He chuckles in my ear, and it's cold and cruel. "Pity you and your baby won't live through the night."

He's going to kill my baby.

Enraged by the thought, I stomp on his foot and elbow him so hard in the ribs that he's forced to let me go. And I run. I run so damn fast I practically fly down the corridor and burst through the doors where...

I come to a grinding halt.

The ER is bustling with activity. Machines beep. Rubber-soled shoes squeak on linoleum. A security guard talking to a nurse stops talking and turns to look at me. I run over to him but I don't get a single word out before the door to the ER bursts open behind me, and I swing around in a panic.

My breath catches in my throat, certain it's going to be the man with the gun.

But it's not. It's a doctor in a white coat rushing into the ER as he talks hurriedly on his phone, obviously talking to the police. "Yes, there are two men dead in the corridor leading into the ER. No, I didn't see anyone else."

The man with the gun must have fled.

"Ma'am, are you okay?" the security guard asks me.

"There are two men in the corridor—they've been shot. There was a man with a gun—"

"A gun?" the nurse gasps.

I shake the security officer's arm. "Please do something."

The security guard talks into his shoulder radio. "We have a possible sighting of the suspect."

He disappears through the doors while the nurse takes my hand.

"You need to sit down."

"But the gunman—"

"Don't worry, the police will find him."

I doubt it. He wasn't just a man with a gun. He was an assassin.

She leads me over to a chair by the nurses' station and leaves to get me some water.

But before she comes back, I hear alarms going off in one of the cubicles across from me. I slowly stand and take slow steps toward it.

The curtain isn't fully closed so I can see a figure on the bed, but I can't make out who it is.

Lev?

The nurse reappears with my water.

"Is that someone from the blast?" I ask desperately.

"I'm sorry, but I'm not at liberty to say," she says, disappearing behind the curtain and yanking it closed.

I'm about to rip the curtain open and demand some answers when a different police officer walks past, and he's talking quickly on his phone. "Yes, two dead in the blast—"

My knees soften.

The pain is swift.

Two dead.

And I suddenly realize I might not want to see what is on the other side of the curtain.

Trembling, I stumble backward to the chair and collapse into it.

Please, no, not Lev.

Not Igor.

The shock sinks in, and I start to cry.

3

BROOKE

I'm going crazy with worry.

After being ushered out of the ER, I'm stuck in my hospital room with a detective who wants to know everything I witnessed.

"Please, do you know anything about Lev or Igor?" I beg him.

But the man standing by my bed doesn't care that I'm losing my mind with worry. He's here to grill me, whether I like it or not.

His name is Detective Blaine Zell, or so he said when he found me crying in the ER and promptly dragged me to my hospital room, telling me I wouldn't be leaving until I gave him a statement.

Five minutes with him and I already don't like him. Since we got back to my room, he's been talking to me like I'm guilty of something.

"Please, you must know something. Are Lev and Igor okay?"

I'm so desperate for news I'm ready to cry again.

But something tells me this guy would get off on it.

"How about we go over your story one more time and then we can find out about your friends," he says, opening up his little notebook again. "So you were at the window when you saw the blast."

"Yes," I huff.

"And then what did you see?"

"Like I've already told you, I saw Lev lying on the ground and a man in a hoodie walking toward him with his gun aimed."

"But this mysterious figure didn't fire the gun."

"No."

"Just pointed it at Mr. Zarkov but didn't shoot?"

Oh my God, douchebag, how many times do we need to go over it? "No."

"And why do you think that is?"

"I *know* why he didn't, it was because two of Lev's men disturbed him when they ran outside, and he walked off."

Detective Zell, a smarmy know-it-all who looks like he might be in his late forties, narrows his eyes at me.

"Tell me again how you knew they were…" He air quotes, "Lev's men."

The fact that he just air-quoted me makes me want to punch him in the face.

"As I've already explained, I know Lev, and I know they are employed by him."

"Remind me, how well do you know Mr. Zarkov?"

This is the second time he's asked how well I know Lev.

The first time I replied with a vague, "Well enough."

This time, I reply with, "I'm his fiancée."

Zell's eyes light up, and then his lips slide into a smirk, and I immediately realize it was a mistake to tell him. Now he's going to grill me harder, drill down as far as he can to get to any of Lev's secrets I might be harboring.

"You're his fiancée—well, congratulations," he says with a fake smile. "I didn't realize the mighty pakhan of the Zarkov Bratva was engaged."

I narrow my eyes at him. "Well, now you do."

He's letting me know he's wise to Lev's association with organized crime. *He's trying to catch me off guard.*

He looks at me like he's trying to crack a code or something. I have a feeling I'm even more of an interest to him now that he knows I am engaged to Lev.

"So this hooded figure disappears, and you run outside into all that mayhem but get pulled back by the two men we found dead in the corridor leading into the ER. Then all three of you get attacked by a mysterious man dressed like an orderly." He laughs like it's ridiculous. "It sounds—"

"Like the truth," I snap. "Because it is."

"I was going to say, frightening."

He wasn't.

He's trying to intimidate me. Trip me up so I'll say something incriminating.

"Listen, can we do this later?" I ask, exhausted by my panic.

"You got somewhere else you need to be?"

"Yes, two people I care about just got blown up."

"Two? There were three."

My eyes dart to him. "What?"

"There were three people."

Who was the third person?

"I overheard a police officer say there were two dead... please, can you tell me if that's true?"

But he just smirks, clearly enjoying my desperation.

Jerk.

"What are you in the hospital for?" he asks.

"That's none of your business." I glower at him. "Look, I told you what I saw. About the hooded figure. About the orderly attacking me and those two men. There is nothing else to tell you."

I throw back the bed covers and swing my legs over the bed. I'm not staying here for another goddamn minute.

"Where do you think you're going?" Zell snarls.

"Since you repeatedly ignore my requests for information about my fiancé and my friend, then I'm going to find out for myself."

"Get back into bed," he growls. But when I don't, he yells, "I said get back into the goddamn bed."

I swing around and bare my gritted teeth at him. I'm about to tell this asshole where to go when the door opens, and a very handsome man in a suit walks in.

"Miss Masters?"

I take in his nice suit and shiny shoes. "Yes?"

"Agent Garrett Michaels with the FBI." He gives me a smile that's right off the pages of a magazine. Perfect white teeth. Dimples. "Is this gentleman harassing you?"

Immediately, Zell's back straightens. "What the fuck—?"

"Leave." The FBI agent doesn't bother to look at him as he issues his dismissal.

But Zell puffs out his chest, ready to take on the alpha dog that's just walked into the room. "Now listen here—"

Agent Michaels swings his bright blue eyes in Zell's direction, and they're blazing with blue fire. "No, you listen here, you fucking ass. I could hear you squawking like a fucking goose all the way down the goddamn hall. This woman is a witness, not a suspect. You hear me? Now, how about you take your little notebook and pen, and go find someone else to annoy. The FBI has jurisdiction on this case, meaning you're no longer needed." He walks to the door and opens it. "That's your clue to leave, asshole."

Zell opens his mouth but closes it again when Agent Michaels levels him with a look of warning.

Put in his place, Zell retreats out of the room, looking butthurt. But not before he issues a threat. "You'll be hearing from my supervisor."

Which doesn't faze the FBI agent one bit.

"I look forward to it. Don't forget to tell him my credentials. Agent Garrett Michaels. Badge number 0266625D."

He closes the door and turns back to me.

"Thank you," I say to him.

He gives me a smile. "You okay?"

"No, Lev and Igor were hurt, and possibly a third person, and no one will tell me if they're alive or dead." My emotion surges forward, bringing tears. "Please, are they dead?"

My hand slides to my belly.

Bracing myself.

Agent Michaels' face is all hard lines and a square jaw, but it softens in the presence of my tears.

"Lev is alive and sedated. He's going to be okay."

The relief rushes over me like a shower of warm water, and I let out a rough exhale. "Oh, thank God."

I rub my belly and let out another deep breath.

"And Igor?"

"He's alive. But he's critical. The odds aren't good."

My relief is quickly followed by a wave of sadness for the friendly giant.

I think of him and Enya in the garden and their stolen glances in and around the mansion. Enya is going to be brokenhearted.

"There was a third person," Agent Michaels says. "He died instantly. He must have been the one to open the car door and take the full force of the explosion. Do you know who it might be?"

One of Lev's men?

Lev mentioned he was going to start training a new driver for me. Could it be him?

I shake my head. "I'm sorry, I don't know."

"Identification is going to be difficult. Considering he's in parts in the morgue."

I frown at Agent Michaels' insensitivity. But I figure you'd have to be a little desensitized as an FBI agent.

"I need to see Lev and Igor," I say, sliding off the bed and reaching for a blanket to wrap around my shoulders.

"You need to rest," Agent Michaels says. "It's been a big twenty-four hours, and you've got the baby to think about."

I spin around to look at him. "How do you know I'm pregnant?"

He smiles and it's not as nice as it was when he first walked in. Now it seems a little... *fake*. "I'm the FBI. I know everything about you, Brooke Rachael Masters, born June 20 to Ivy and Michael Masters."

My spine begins to tingle, and I swallow thickly. I don't think Agent Michaels is the ally I thought he was. "What do you want?"

"I just want to talk."

"I need to see Lev."

I try to move past him, but he puts out a hand to stop me.

"In time, you can see him, but before then, you and I need to talk."

Frustrated, I snap. "Sorry, but I'm all talked out about the explosion tonight."

I'm going to find Lev, and no one, not even this blue-eyed titan, is going to stop me.

"I don't want to talk about the explosion," he says, removing a tray of nicotine gum from the breast pocket of his jacket and popping a piece of gum into his mouth.

I look at him, surprised. "You don't?"

He shakes his head, and those bright blue eyes sharpen on me.

"No, Miss Masters. I want to put Lev Zarkov behind bars for his crimes. And you're going to help me do it."

4
LEV

It hurts like a motherfucker.

I'm riding a wave of pain when I wake up. The pounding in my skull feels like I'm being pistol-whipped. My eyelids are heavy and hard to open, and when I do, all I can see is hazy white light. I move, and every muscle in my body protests.

I groan, wondering what the fuck happened.

Then I remember the explosion.

Igor, Victor, and I were walking to the car. I was talking on the phone to Brooke...

Brooke.

I sit up and wince at the pain.

My head feels broken.

But I push past the pain.

I need to get to Brooke.

To protect her.

That's when I remember the baby, and I feel a rush of anger sweep through me. Anger at Vlad. Anger at Vadim. Anger at me for not seeing this coming.

The fury I feel pouring into my veins overrides the pain in my head, and I rip off the cords stuck to my chest and belly that tether me to the heart monitor, and pull out the needle in my arm attached to the IV.

I have to find Brooke.

And Igor.

I know there is no chance Victor made it. The last I saw of him, he was opening the car door.

I stumble out of the bed. I'm still dressed in my button-up shirt and suit pants, but they're a mess from being thrown backward into the flower garden. My shoes are missing, and my gun is gone. Looking around, I find my shoes on a chair beside the bed, but I must be on some crazy heavy drugs because I can barely stand up straight.

"Hey, you shouldn't be out of bed," a nurse says as she walks into the ER cubicle. "You have a concussion. Not to mention a couple of bruised ribs."

Like I can't feel the pain radiating out of my body like I'm on fire.

"I have to find Brooke." My mouth feels like it's full of cotton wool. "I have to find my fiancée."

"That will have to wait," the nurse says. She tries to guide me back toward the bed, but I brush past her, only to walk into the police officer posted outside of the cubicle.

And he's a big motherfucker.

"You ain't going anywhere," he says.

"Where is my gun?"

"You'll get it back when you're released," the nurse says, walking toward me with a syringe in her hand.

I try to dodge out of her way, but my feet are too heavy.

I also try to push past the police officer, but he doesn't move, and I'm too drugged to fight him. I try but my arms are useless, and it only pisses him off.

So I use my voice. Issue some threats. Growl out obscenities.

Until I feel the sharp sting of the needle, and I am sent into oblivion once again.

When I open my eyes again, I'm in a hospital room, and Brooke's sweet face is the first thing I see. Immediately, a soothing warmth settles over me from head to toe.

"Hey," she says gently, curling her fingers around mine.

"Are you okay?" I ask.

She smiles softly. "Aren't I supposed to be asking you that?"

"I'm alive. That's a good sign." I reach for her. I'm desperate to hold her. But the moment I lift my arms, an agonizing pain rockets through my torso. *Bruised ribs. Fucking great.*

Brooke puts her arm out to stop me. "Lev—"

"I'm okay." I pull her into my arms, and the soft cloud of her scent is an instant comfort. I press a kiss into her hair and hold her there for a moment before letting her go. "And the baby?"

"Our baby is fine."

Our baby.

Even through the murkiness of medication, those words send something pure and right into my heart.

The clock on the wall behind Brooke reads five-seventeen, but I'm so disoriented I don't know if it's day or night. "Is it morning or night?"

"It's morning. The blast happened last night. They sedated you. Feliks was here. He said to call him when you wake up, and he'll be back. He said to let you know he's holding down the fort, but you'd better stop sleeping on the job and get your ass out of bed."

Fucking Feliks.

I press my fingers to my eyes and rub. I'm so bone-tired it doesn't feel like I've slept. "Where is Igor?"

Immediately, Brooke's face falls, and she hesitates, so I know I'm not going to like the answer.

"He's alive, but it doesn't look good, Lev. He's on life support."

The news hits me hard, and I feel it right down to my marrow.

"The doctors said it's a miracle he's still alive. That anyone half his size…" She catches a sob in her throat, and her eyes brim with tears.

I sit up, ignoring the protest from my bruised ribs, and swing my legs over the side of the bed.

Thankfully, I'm not as heavily medicated as I was in the ER, and my legs actually support me when I climb off the bed.

"Should you be doing this?" Brooke asks, even though she knows it's pointless. She knows by now there's no point in trying to stop me when I get an idea in my head.

"If they stop drugging me, I'll be fine. Which room is he in?"

"He's in the burn unit."

Her words punch me in the gut.

Burn unit.

Fuck.

It's hard to keep the edge from my voice. "Show me."

She hesitates and then nods.

It's slow going as I follow her through the hospital corridors on unstable feet. But after several exhausting and agonizing minutes, we arrive outside Igor's hospital room. We can see Igor through a viewing window. He's unconscious on the bed, covered head to toe in bandages with a breathing tube in his mouth.

When I see him, I have to steady myself against the wall. I've known Igor since he started working as my father's chauffeur twenty years ago. I was a bratty teenager, and he was somewhere in his twenties. He's not just a Zarkov employee. He's fucking family.

My jaw tightens, and I grit my teeth so hard my jawbone aches.

I'm going to find those responsible for this, and I'm going to break every single one of their bones slowly.

My hands fist at my side.

Brooke notices and slides a comforting hand up and down my back. It's the only thing that stops me from pounding the wall with my fist.

When a doctor approaches Igor's room, I stop him. "What's the update?"

"Are you family?"

"Yes," I lie easily. "Is he going to live?"

"It's too early to tell. He's suffered numerous injuries that are fatal on their own. Abdominal hemorrhage and perforation. Injuries to his lungs and gastrointestinal tract. Then there's the broken pelvis and lacerations from flying debris. He also has burns to thirty percent of his body."

The beast inside me roars to life, and it takes everything I can to tame it. Outwardly, I'm a statue. But internally, the beast is struggling to break free from my restraint. He wants out, and he wants revenge. *Badly.*

I hate the fear I hear in my voice. "Will he survive?"

"Perhaps. But he's not out of the woods yet. Actually, he's far from it. If he makes it through the day, it will be a miracle."

"And if he does?"

"Then we take one day at a time. His injuries are so severe, he's going to be in rehabilitation for a long while."

I turn to look at Igor lying on the bed and feel the rage burn like fire in my gut.

"I want him to receive the best care. Do you hear me? The best specialists. The best everything. I don't care if I have to send planes all over the world to pick up those specialists and bring them back here. I will."

"I understand your concern. But he's in good hands. Some of the best specialists in the world are in this hospital. You can trust us to look after him." He nods toward the nurses' station. "We've been trying to find out who he was. His wallet and identification were burned up in the blast. Since you're family, you'll need to fill out the necessary paperwork. Insurance. Sign a care plan. After that, you need to go home and get some rest. You look like you could use it."

I nod absentmindedly as I watch my friend fight for his life on the other side of the window.

But I beg to differ. I'm not going home to rest.

First things first.

I'm going to get my gun back.

And then I'm going to shell out some payback.

5

BROOKE

"The doctor is right—you need to come home," I say.

We've just signed all the necessary paperwork for Igor and discharged ourselves. Since then, Lev's been glued to his phone as we wait for Feliks to pick us up, issuing orders in Russian to his men.

"I'll take you home, but I need to move swiftly on this."

"You have a concussion and bruised ribs," I remind him.

"It's a mild concussion, and I'm not going to waste time crying over a couple of bruised ribs. I need to gather my men, and we need to act now."

"Lev—"

"I've already wasted too much time in the hospital. I've lost the night. Who knows what these motherfuckers have been able to get away with while I was out cold in a hospital bed."

He knows about the orderly attacking me. When I told him, he went very still, and the muscle in his jaw ticked, and he drew in a deep breath through flared nostrils. It's like he was so enraged he didn't dare move in case it detonated that part of him that was already barely in control.

It took me talking to him calmly and reassuring him that neither the baby nor I were hurt before he could even speak. But even then, I knew it had ignited something inside him. Something dark and powerful and capable of more than I could even imagine.

But I haven't had a chance to tell him about Agent Michaels because every time I open my mouth to tell him, his phone rings, and he starts barking orders into the phone, organizing people to do things I don't really understand.

"Lev, I need to tell you something," I say as we walk toward the hospital exit. "The FBI came and saw me."

He stops typing a message on his phone and looks up. He thinks for a minute, then says, "Let me guess, a six-foot-two clown with blue eyes and ice-white teeth who goes by the name of Agent Michaels?"

"You know him?"

For the first time since he woke up, he manages a smile. "He's had a hard-on for me for a long time. I call him my shadow. He's nothing to worry about."

I can't believe how nonchalant he's being. I thought this information was going to fuel his rage. That's why I didn't mention it when I told him about the orderly who attacked me. I didn't want to inflame an already catastrophic situation.

I can't help but look surprised. "He's not a threat?"

"If I see Agent Michaels as a threat, then I have no business being pakhan. He's an egotistical pen pusher who is more interested in being an FBI golden boy than having the balls to actually take me on. You have nothing to worry about. I'm good at what I do, *zayka*. He'll never be able to pin anything on me unless someone in my inner circle betrays me and tells him everything he wants to know." His face suddenly grows serious, and his dark brows pull in. "He didn't threaten you, did he?"

"No, but he tried to intimidate me and did a really good job of it."

Lev's face softens. "You have nothing to be intimidated about. He's got nothing on me."

"What if someone talks?"

He runs his hands down my arms. "No one is talking. No one would dare."

But I can't help but feel uneasy about the FBI agent.

"Lev, he makes me nervous. He knew everything about me. About my parents. Where I grew up. Our baby."

Lev's jaw clenches, and I can see it in his eyes. He will set Agent Michaels alight if he dares to fuck with me and this baby.

Despite his bruised body, Lev pulls me into his chest and wraps his arms around me. "I don't want you worrying about this." He pulls back to cup my face. "I'm going to protect you and our baby."

He kisses me, and it's tender and reassuring, and I drink it in. *Needing it.*

He skims his thumb across my cheek. "You're safe now. Even if the world burns down around you, where you stand will be safe."

He presses a kiss to my forehead just as Feliks walks into the hospital.

He's not smiling, and it's odd seeing him so uptight.

"You look like shit," he says to Lev.

As usual, Lev downplays it. "It's nothing."

Feliks turns to me, and his face softens when he sees my bruises. "We need to get you home so you can rest."

"I'm fine," I say.

He doesn't know about the baby. Lev and I have agreed to keep quiet about it for now. There is a lot going on, and a lot more is about to start.

"Still, you look like you need to put your feet up. Come on, I've got a car waiting out the front. Don't worry, I brought a soldier with me. He'll make sure we don't find any more surprises waiting for us when we open the car doors."

Lev takes my hand and leads me out of the hospital.

Outside, dawn is breaking on the horizon, but the morning is warm. Summer is coming.

"I see your shadow is here," Feliks says as we walk to the car. I follow his line of sight and see the black car in the parking lot, sitting beneath a streetlight. The windows are up, but I can see someone inside. A cold shiver runs up my back.

Agent Michaels.

Why does he make me so uneasy?

Because when he told you he wanted your help to take down Lev, he went on to dangle your old life in front of you. And for one nanosecond, he had you wishing you were back living in it, because in your old life there were no Vlads, or kidnappings, or guns and car bombs.

I push the memory of our conversation back.

That might be true, but this is the world I live in now, whether I like it or not. Not because of my growing feelings for Lev—hell, I'm not even sure what they are—but because of the baby growing in my belly.

The heir.

"Brooke has already had the pleasure of meeting him," Lev tells Feliks.

Feliks pulls a face as he opens the door for me. "As if you hadn't already been through enough today."

I slide onto the back seat. There's a man in the driver's seat who I guess is the soldier Feliks mentioned. Added security to make sure no more car tampering took place.

Lev slides in beside me while Feliks takes the front.

"I want a tail on the shadow as of this minute," Lev says. "I want to know where he is and who he's talking to. And we're going to increase security tenfold."

Turning my head to the window, I stare out into the growing sunlight.

If I already thought the constant presence of security and bodyguards was exhausting, now it's only going to get worse.

6
LEV

I hate leaving her. Because no one can protect her like I can.

But I have to take action now, so I double the security in and around the Zarkov Estate, and by the time we arrive home, there are already more men patrolling the inner walls.

Inside the mansion, Brooke makes her way through the foyer.

"I need to sleep," she says wearily.

I follow her up the grand staircase, but when she turns right to go to her bedroom, I take her by the wrists.

"No, from now on, you sleep in my room with me."

She looks surprised. "Isn't that breaking the rules?"

I slide my hands inside hers. "There are no rules now. We're at war, and I intend to protect you and the baby the best way I can. When you sleep, it is with me, in my bed."

She looks up at me, the expression on her bruised face full of uncertainty, and it crushes me to see the fear in her big brown eyes.

I trace a finger along her eyebrow and down her cheeks, then cup her jaw in my hands. "The worst is behind us."

I know it's a bold statement. But she needs to know I will do everything in my power to ensure she will never have to endure any more time in the hands of my enemies.

I kiss her, and it's shaky and broken because we're both bruised and tattered, but as we stand there in the dim light of the hallway, our kiss is a reminder that amongst the bloodshed and the shadows of war, we still have *this*.

It doesn't matter that we don't know what *this* is.

For now, it is enough.

And it is perfect.

I take her to my bedroom, and she stops in the doorway and casts an astonished gaze around the room.

"It's so beautiful," she whispers.

My bedroom is over-the-top opulent. A bedroom fit for a king. Large, with cathedral ceilings and a bed so massive it needs custom-made sheets.

Now that I am in the sanctuary of my own room, I feel the weight of the last forty-eight hours in every cell and neuron in my body.

"Do you need to shower?" I ask.

She nods, and I lead her into the colossal marble bathroom off the bedroom. In the dim light, I slowly peel the clothes from her, my gut tightening when I see her bruises up close.

She starts to undo my shirt buttons, and I stop her.

"Let me look after you," I say.

"This *is* you looking after me," she whispers. "Join me in the shower. Hold me. Kiss me."

Despite my bruised ribs and the ache in every muscle of my body, I harden at the sight of her nakedness. But tonight is not about sex. It's about being here together. I want to soothe her, not fuck her. Although my cock is pretty certain we could do both.

In the shower, she hisses in a breath when the water hits the cut to her lip and the injuries on her beautiful face, so I turn her away from it and angle her head so the warm water runs down her long hair.

"Better?"

"Thank you," she moans.

I take my time with her. Lathering her body in soap and washing the suds from her skin. I want to wash away every moment she endured at the hand of Vlad. From his abusive touch to his vile, brutal energy, I don't want any of it lingering on her flesh. I want to soothe her and comfort her.

And when my hands slide over her flat belly, the thought of my baby sends an overwhelming need to protect them both to the most primal parts of me.

I will do anything to keep them safe.

Turning her in my arms to face me, I hold her and kiss her.

She reaches between us, her warm hands taking hold of my slippery cock.

"Zayka—"

"I almost lost you last night," she says gently as she starts to stroke me. "I need this. *You* need this."

My cock throbs with agreement in her skillful hands. And despite the pain in my body, my balls grow heavy and swell with arousal with every sensual stroke.

I take her face in my hands and kiss her slowly as the pleasure rises in me. I groan into her mouth, wanting her, needing to bury myself so deep in her that I forget everything in the outside world.

But bruised ribs are a motherfucker, and even I have to admit defeat. Fucking her against the tiles is not going to happen tonight.

But I can make her come in other ways.

As she continues to stroke me, I press her back to the wall dripping with shower water and slide my fingers between her thighs where she's slick and ready for me. She bites down on her wet lips, droplets of water spilling from her long eyelashes as she looks up at me.

God, she's so beautiful.

I can't help it. I crush my lips to hers, hard and demanding, but remember her bruised, split lip and pull away.

"No," she pants desperately. "Kiss me."

She yanks me back to her mouth, her tongue sweeping in, and I groan at the pleasure.

Her hands slip along my cock, water squelching with every stroke.

She whimpers as I rub her clit, and it's almost my undoing.

"Oh God, *zayka*—" I bite back the need to come. Because I need to get her there first.

She sags against the wall, her strokes faltering as her body softens, and she begins to tremble and moan.

My cock aches with the loss of friction, and pain be damned, I let her have her orgasm, but before she finishes, I hoist up her leg and thrust into her wet pussy and take my own. Everything hurts, but it's nothing compared to the pleasure of chasing an orgasm and then coming inside her.

Except this time, I know she's pregnant with my baby, and there is something primal in my release. It's me claiming her. *Claiming them.*

My chest heaving, I slip out of her warm body and press my forehead to hers, kissing her wet lips until both our breathing evens out.

When we're done, we step out of the shower, and I carefully dry her off, taking special care of her bruises.

"I'm a lot stronger than you think," she says softly.

And I don't know why, but a rush of pride and admiration pours into my chest.

But it's quickly followed by a guilt so gut-wrenching it physically hurts. She shouldn't have to reassure me of her strength. None of this should have happened.

"Wait here," I say, wrapping her in a towel before leaving the bathroom. In my dressing room, I quickly slide on a fresh pair of black pants and a belt before grabbing one of my shirts for Brooke.

When I return to the bathroom, she's combing her long hair.

I come up behind her and meet her eyes in the enormous mirror, and that familiar jolt of pain grips me when I see her bruised face. I swallow thickly.

"I won't break, I promise," she adds, clearly reading my emotions like a book, something she's getting good at. "I can move on from this."

But her words gut me. She shouldn't have to.

There is a hairdryer in one of the drawers. I remove it and start drying her hair, wanting to take care of every inch of her.

It's not lost on me that I should be elsewhere.

That I should be corralling my men and preparing for retaliation.

But right now, I'm needed here, and seeing Brooke's sweet face looking at me in the reflection of the mirror, I know where I'd rather be.

Here with my fiancée and my baby.

"Can I get you a drink?" I ask after I've dried off her hair.

She shakes her head. "I'm too tired. I just need to sleep."

She climbs into bed, and I crawl onto the bed beside her.

I'm so damn tired, and every muscle in my body aches to fall asleep with her in my arms. To listen to her soft breathing and let myself sink into the inky darkness of sleep.

But I need to keep her and the baby safe, and my lying here indulging in the comfort of her soft warmth is not going to make that happen.

War starts today. And it is going to be bloody and violent.

Not that I tell her that. I keep those thoughts to myself. And if she asks questions, I will downplay my responses so I don't scare her, just like I downplayed the threat of Agent Michaels to Brooke because I need to protect her.

The truth is, Agent Michaels is a giant pain in the ass. Ever since I became pakhan, he's been trying to find something to pin on me. He's poked around in almost everything I am involved in. My business affairs. My financial affairs. My personal life. Obviously, he's found nothing, but he's like a dog with a bone, and he's not going to stop until I'm in jail or he's dead. And after learning about Brooke's encounter with him, I'm contemplating the latter.

I wasn't lying to Brooke when I said he won't get anything on me. I move in circles that are unforgiving toward those who talk to the authorities, and I never leave any witnesses.

Well, except Wilson.

He's the exception.

He's only alive because Brooke gave up her freedom for his life.

But if anyone were stupid enough to open their mouths... well, things could get very tricky for me. Even with the swift hand of the bratva behind me, damage could be done before we brought it under control.

But today, I have bigger fish to fry.

Today, I'm going to decimate Vlad and everything dear to him. His business. His home. His car collection. *His entire everything.*

But for now, I'm going to wait until Brooke falls asleep.

And then ensure the impenetrable wall of security will keep her safe when I'm gone.

She reaches for me, and I hold her, waiting for that sweet lullaby of her sleeping breath. But it doesn't come.

"I know you have to leave," she says quietly. "But can you just stay with me a while?"

I think about the war I'm about to unleash on Vlad. But how can I leave her when she needs me?

My men know what I need from them today. They can gather the arsenal I need while I stay where I am needed the most. I will push back my urge for bloodshed and focus on Brooke's needs.

Today can wait.

Right now is for her.

7
LEV

The Zarkov Bratva.

A family born from blood, sweat, and power sit around the war table in the basement of ZeeMed headquarters.

The inner sanctum consists of the twelve men who were loyal to my father and now to me: my uncles—Boris and Vadim, my cousin Maksim, and, of course, my most trusted Feliks. Our soldiers, of which there are thousands, do not attend these meetings. This is where the decisions are made. This is where war is declared.

When Feliks and I walk in, the energy in the room is tense. Every man is ready to respond to what Vlad has done with uninhibited force.

Taking my place at the head of the table, I'm ready to address the issue at hand. But when I see Vadim sitting there like he doesn't have a fucking care in the world, I have to bite back the urge to pull out my gun and demand he tell me how involved he is with Vlad.

Luckily for him, drawing a weapon during one of these meetings would be breaking a long-standing rule. But that doesn't stop the blood heating in my veins or dampen the urge to put a bullet between his eyes.

I don't know if Vadim has a secretive alliance with Vlad or if he is, in fact, the one pulling Vlad's strings, but I am sure he is involved somehow. Did he have Brooke kidnapped? Was he the one who ordered the car bombing? The hairs on the back of my neck stand on end, and I have to remind myself that there are ways to do things, and shooting my uncle in the face for his betrayal is not it. Well, not today.

It might actually be good he's here.

Because right now, I don't know how deep his disloyalty runs, but after today, I will. He's not leaving until I find out the goddamn truth.

Further down the table, I notice two chairs are empty. Boris and Maksim. I frown and drum my fingers against the table. I didn't expect Vadim to show his guilty face. But Boris and Maksim's absence is surprising.

"You look well, Pakhan," says an older vor. "It was a blessing you were not injured as badly as our dear friend Igor."

"Is Igor expected to live?" another vor asks.

Feliks replies, "Igor is as strong as an ox. He will survive."

I think of my friend swathed in bandages and fighting for his life in a hospital bed, and my gaze slides to Vadim. He will pay for what he has done.

"Vlad Bhyzova declared war on this bratva when he kidnapped my fiancée and then attempted to assassinate me. Since then, it appears he's fled underground. I've called you all here today because I intend to smoke him out…" My eyes lock with Vadim's. "…and whoever he may be working with."

"Who would be dumb enough?" an old vor at the end of the table scoffs.

"Do we know who might be working with him?" another vor asks.

Again, my gaze moves to Vadim. "I have a fair idea."

Vadim frowns. "And who would that be?"

My eyes narrow. "Why don't you tell me your theories, Uncle?"

"Vlad Bhyzova is a *mudak*. He couldn't orchestrate a fuck in a brothel. If he did what you said he did—"

I grit my teeth. "He put Brooke in the hospital after he kidnapped and beat her."

"Then my condolences to your bride-to-be, Nephew. But Vlad isn't smart enough to do this alone. Someone else must be driving the machine."

"My thoughts exactly," I growl.

He has the nerve to look indignant as he asks, "You think it's me?"

"If it looks like a rat and smells like a rat, then it must be—"

"My acquaintance with Vlad does not extend to an alliance."

I bang my fist on the table. "Enough with the lies. You and Vlad have been working together."

"I am not working with him. Vlad Bhyzova is of no use to me."

I stand and stalk down the table toward him. Then breaking the sanctity of the inner sanctum, I pull out my gun and point it at my uncle. *Rules be damned.* "Lie to me again, and I'll shoot you in the fucking head."

His eyebrows shoot up. "Just like you did to Aleks?"

"*Exactly* like I did to Aleks. You betray the bratva like he did, and you die like he did."

He slowly rises to his feet but makes no move for the gun I know he keeps in the breast pocket of his suit. "You are out of control."

"Which is the right thing to say to a man pointing his fucking gun at you," I growl.

The door opens, and Boris and Maksim stroll in as if they're not fifteen fucking minutes late.

"Looks like we're missing out on all the fun," Boris jokes, but his smile quickly fades when he feels the fury burning off me like flames.

"What the hell is going on?" Maksim asks.

"Perhaps we should sit down," Boris says to his son and ushers him to their seats.

"Good fucking idea. You can tell me why you were late once I've dealt with this *mudak* and his scheme to get rid of me so he could step into the role of pakhan."

Vadim remains stoic, looking down the barrel of my gun. "That's not true."

"No? You've been scheming to get rid of me since I stepped into this role. Always questioning my decisions. Whispering behind my back, knowing it would get back to me."

"It's no secret I think you're too young for the role. I've never tried to hide it." He looks to his brother, but Boris looks away. "But I would not betray my pakhan."

"Then explain to me why every time I turn around, I find you and Vlad together."

His eyes sparkle back at me, and for a moment, I can see my father in them. A proud, intelligent man and a brilliant strategist.

My grip on my gun tightens.

He is nothing like my father.

"Vlad is an associate, nothing more. You will need to trust me on this, Nephew."

I step closer. "But I don't trust you, *Uncle*. I want you gone."

"You don't have any proof to have me thrown out of this bratva. I'm not Aleks. I'm a part of the inner circle. The rules apply."

An old vor clears his throat. "Vadim is correct, Pakhan. There are ways to do these things. I urge you to put down your gun."

"And I want answers," I growl. I press my gun to Vadim's temple, and the tension in the room gets heavier. "Fuck the rules."

Vadim looks to Boris. "You have nothing to say, Brother?"

But Boris remains tight-lipped, and Vadim sends him a menacing look.

He closes his eyes.

But I don't pull the trigger. Instead, I rip my gun away and step close enough to whisper in his ear, "You're lucky I want answers more than I want your brains splattered all over this table."

The proud old man's shoulders sag with relief, but he says nothing.

I turn my attention to Feliks, Boris, and Maksim. "In my office, now. The rest of you are dismissed."

I don't mention Brooke's pregnancy. For now, she has a large enough target on her back because she is my fiancée. I can only imagine how big that target would grow when my enemies learn she is carrying my heir.

8
LEV

"Well, that was intense," Feliks says as the four of us ride the elevator from the basement to my office on the penthouse floor.

"Did you follow up on those things I asked you to look into?" I ask him.

Feliks has been on Vlad detail, and I want to know everything. Where he was last seen. When his credit cards were last used. We have eyes on his house and other properties that he has around New York and across the country, and I've had my men leave no stone unturned looking for him.

If he's smart, he would've left New York by now.

Feliks leans against the mirrored elevator wall. Relaxed as usual. "I did. But why are we going to your apartment? I could just as easily have filled you in downstairs."

I ignore his question. "And what did you find out?"

"His credit cards haven't been used since the day following the attack on Brooke. And he hasn't been seen in just as long. He hasn't stepped foot in any of his properties here in New York or anywhere else. But we're still looking."

I turn my attention to Boris and Maksim. I'm pissed at them for arriving late to the meeting. Their tardiness is disrespectful and unacceptable, not to mention suspicious. It might be paranoia, but I'm not beyond suspecting my closest family members at this stage. "Where were you?"

"No disrespect was meant, Nephew," Boris says. "But we had a lead on Vlad that we needed to pursue. It was time-sensitive. We had to act on it."

"He'd been keeping company with a woman in New Jersey in the lead-up to the attack on Brooke," Maksim explains. "We were lead to believe he might be holed up with her."

"Who told you this?"

Boris clears his throat rather sheepishly. "A friend."

I glare at my uncle. "And who is this friend?"

"A dancer by the name of Brandi-Lynn. She works at—"

"The Pink Diamond," I interrupt.

Boris's eyes light up. "You know her?"

I shoot him another glare. "No. It was an easy guess, knowing your penchant for girls at The Pink Diamond."

Boris offers me another sheepish grin.

"And this Brandi-Lynn, how would she know about Vlad and where he's hiding out?" I ask, growing impatient.

Feeling my mood, Maksim explains, "Another dancer confided in her. Told her she was spending time with him. Said he had plans to make a move on some big players in town. He told her she was fucking the man who would be King of New York by the end of the month."

Boris adds, "According to Brandi-Lynn, Vlad was planning on taking some, quote, 'Russian cunt's bride' and making him pay for her safe return."

My hands curl into fists, and I clench my teeth. When I think about what Vlad did to Brooke, how he marked her skin, how terrified she must have been... I have to breathe in slowly through my nose to calm the rising fire in me. "And when you visited this woman in New Jersey, what happened?"

Boris looks frustrated. "It was a complete waste of our time."

Maksim adds, "Vlad wasn't there. She said she hadn't seen him in days."

"And you believed her?"

"When she showed us the burned pile of his belongings in the back yard, we did. She thought he'd run off with another woman, so she set fire to any clothes or belongings he'd left at her apartment."

The elevator reaches the penthouse suite, and when the doors open, I'm first to leave. I step into my office and head straight to the bar to pour a shot of vodka. I need to calm the angry beast inside of me. It wants loose, and it wants to roar. I'm used to being in control, but right now, I feel my grip on it slipping away because I'm so angry I want to burn the entire world down. *Because of what was done to her and my failure to stop it from happening.*

"Lev, why are we in your apartment?" Maksim asks. "This is information we could've shared at the meeting."

I don't sip the vodka. I down it in one mouthful. "Because, as of this moment, you three are the only three people I trust."

My uncle and cousins share confused looks.

I walk over to the floor-to-ceiling windows overlooking the city. "How did Vlad know Brooke was going to be at that liquor store?"

"He must have had somebody watching her," Boris says.

I turn to look at him. "Perhaps, but this feels more than opportunistic. This feels planned. He had a point to make. He wanted to show that he could get to me and my circle whenever he wanted to. He waited for the right opportunity, and when it presented itself, he was ready. But he doesn't have the resources to have men on constant surveillance."

Maksim frowns. "You think someone in the bratva told him?"

The idea makes me sick. "Yes, I think we have a rat in the house. And I don't mean Vadim. Whoever took her knew where she was going to be."

Feliks' brows pull together. "There was only a handful of people who knew Brooke was going to be there. You, me, Maksim, Igor, and the new bodyguard."

I turn back to the view below. "The new bodyguard who was with her the day she was taken. What do we know about him?"

"He's ex-military. He was vetted well. He's straight down the line."

But he's new.

We vet soldiers rigorously. We leave no stone unturned when it comes to their past and their associations. But trust needs to be earned. And I don't know him, so I don't trust him. And I'm fucking angry at myself for putting Brooke in his charge.

"Tell Pierce I want the bodyguard looked into." My head of security is like a bloodhound. If there is anything fishy in the bodyguard's life, he'll find it. "I want every minute detail of his life looked into. If he's the rat, something is going to prove he's tied to Vlad somehow."

"And if he is, you want me to dispose of him?" Feliks asks.

"No, I will do it myself. People need to learn that if they touch my fiancée, then I'm gonna make sure there's hell to pay."

9
LEV

After I leave my uncle and cousins, I head to the hospital to check in on Igor.

The nurse is changing his bandages when I arrive, so I stand at the viewing window, my body tense with anger. It hurts to see my friend lying there.

I feel a person next to me, and when I look, it's Agent Michaels.

"The doctor says it's a miracle he survived," Michaels says.

I feel the hairs on the back of my neck curl. Being this close to my shadow is like standing next to a toxic cloud of radioactive matter. "Are you intimidating medical staff to give you information now?"

"I'm a federal agent, Zarkov. You'd be surprised what a flash of credentials will get me."

I look away from him to focus on Igor and tell myself that a hospital ward is not the place to shoot a federal agent.

"There's going to be a thorough investigation into the explosion. A lot of rocks are going to be turned over. Every nook and cranny will be looked into. Things are going to get quite difficult for you and your men."

I don't take the bait and keep staring straight ahead.

"The bureau won't stop until they get answers, Zarkov."

Again, I don't take the bait. I ignore him and keep my eyes focused ahead. In my experience, the easiest way to ensure no one trips you up in conversation is to not say anything at all.

"Your fiancée is quite lovely," he says.

But then he goes and says that.

So I take the bait, because Michaels needs to know that he can fuck with all the other areas of my life—I have enough men and power that it will never worry me. But when it comes to Brooke, she is completely off limits.

I turn to look at him. "You stay away from her."

He smirks. "Afraid your relationship is shaky enough that she might say something she shouldn't?"

Surprising him, I grab him by the collar and shove him up against the wall.

"Go ahead, Zarkov. I'm a federal agent. Keep giving me cause to arrest you. It will be my pleasure to bring you in and file charges against you."

His threat isn't enough to make me let go. I pull him a little bit closer so we're eye to eye, our faces inches from each other. "You listen to me, you ambitious little fuck. You can poke around all you want into my life. You wanna waste your time, go for it. But you go anywhere near Brooke again, and all bets are off. Those FBI credentials will not be able to protect you from me."

I let him go, and he straightens his collar. At least he has the good sense to look rattled, even if he's trying hard not to show it.

"That's your one and only warning," I growl.

I walk away before I do something stupid. Like put a bullet in his head.

Although, he makes a compelling argument for me to do it.

I want to get home to Brooke, but as I pass the waiting room, I see Enya curled up in a chair, biting her thumbnail, her eyes red from crying.

When she sees me walk in, she uncurls her legs and stands up. "Pakhan—"

I gesture for her to sit down. "You look tired. Have you been here all night?"

"Yes, the nurses told me to go home to get some sleep, but I can't leave him here. He's so alone."

She looks exhausted. "Have you eaten?"

"They keep the vending machine well stocked."

"Come back to the house with me. You need a hot meal and some rest."

"No, I can't leave him."

Her sweet features are marred by fear and sadness. "You really care about him, don't you?"

She forces a smile just as more tears spill out of her eyes. "I've had a crush on him for years. I didn't think anything would ever happen. It wasn't until Brooke came along that everything fell into place." She sobs. "Now it doesn't look like he's going to make it, and all I can think about is all the time we wasted. All the things we haven't done. All the things we could've done but never did. Because we were both afraid to say how we truly feel."

I get it.

We take time for granted. But when time begins to run out, it becomes the most important thing in the world.

I think of Brooke waiting for me at home, and I'm overcome with an intense need to see her.

"He's going to make it, Enya. And you'll get all your futures with him."

She nods, but it's the weary nod of a loved one who has been pacing the hospital waiting room and halls for days.

"I wish I had your confidence," she says.

I scoff silently. If only my confidence were real.

I drive home too fast, my thoughts heavy after seeing Igor.

But the moment I step into my room and find Brooke waiting for me in my bed, my tension eases a little.

I fall into bed beside her and let my sweet bratva lullaby soothe my aching heart.

∼

I wake up in a cold sweat and with a racing heart. Instinctively, I reach for Brooke in the darkness, needing her comforting touch. She stirs and twists her body around to face me.

"Lev?" she murmurs sleepily.

"It's okay, *zayka*, I'm sorry I woke you."

She nestles closer to me and runs her fingers softly along my jaw. "Did you have a nightmare?"

I did, and its rattled me. A cold shiver snakes its way down my back. I had dreamed about a car bomb and then about a world without Brooke in it, and my heart had obliterated when I realized I would never see her, or get to touch her, or hold her, or make love to her again.

I pull her closer and secure her in my arms.

A world without her in it would be cold and unforgiving and—

Fuck. I let out a rough breath. It was just a nightmare, for fuck's sake.

But no matter how much I try to shake it off, the eerie feeling sticks to me like an unseen cobweb.

Brooke's arm snakes around my waist, and she buries her face into my chest, and the comfort it brings is unmeasurable.

"Do you want to talk about it?" she murmurs, her lips brushing against my skin.

"No," I rasp, as her hand trails down my abs to brush against my cock.

She starts to softly stroke her fingertips along the heavy shaft, and a sweet pleasure begins to unfurl.

"Tell me what your dream was about," she murmurs.

I roll her onto her back. I don't want to talk about it. I don't want her to know the level of fear I feel when I think of a world without her. I want to fuck it out of my head and then some.

I climb over her and settle between her legs. But Brooke places her hands on my chest and pushes me back. She's wide awake now, looking up at me. "Lev—"

My cock is ready, and I inch it toward her pussy. "It's nothing."

But Brooke isn't having it. "It's not nothing."

I take my cock by the base, but Brooke shakes her head.

"Stop." Her big eyes search my face. "Talk to me, Lev."

With a dissatisfied grunt, I roll off her and slump back into the pillows. I lie on my back and look up at the ceiling for what seems like the millionth fucking time tonight. It's the first time she's denied me, and I don't love it.

She leans up on her elbow and gently caresses my chest with featherlike fingertips, which is soothing to both my mood and the unease left behind by my nightmare.

"What was the dream about?" she asks.

Another fractured image of her dying in an explosion and me having to hold her in my arms as she dies quietly guts me. It's like my stomach is twisting in on itself, and the pain is excruciating.

"It was nothing." I try brushing it off. "I don't even remember it."

Of course, she knows I'm lying. But I'm not going to scare her with a crazy dream about her perishing and me falling apart because of it.

"Let me in," she says quietly, her big eyes soft and full of concern. "Tell me what's on your mind."

"Fucking you into tomorrow, which, incidentally, I was about to do."

She lifts an eyebrow and gives me a very pointed look. "You know what I mean."

I let out a rough exhale and drag my fingers down my face. I know that look. Neither of us is going back to sleep until she's satisfied I'm not keeping anything from her. I rub both my eyes with my fingers and concede I might as well give her something so we can both go back to sleep.

"You left me and never came back," I say, struggling over the words. "You and the baby were gone."

She puts her palms on either side of my face and looks into my eyes. "Me and the baby are right here, Lev. You can't get rid of us that easily."

She kisses me, deep and so sweet like she is drawing my pain from inside me and drinking it from my lips. And she keeps kissing me, even when I roll onto her and push inside her parted thighs and stroke deep into her body. And when my hips begin to thrust harder and faster, still she keeps kissing me, drawing my pain from me like she's vanquishing a demon from my body.

I try to come. Need to come. But I can't. And finally, my frustration peaks, and I let out a frustrated roar.

She looks up at me, and our eyes connect, and out of nowhere, my wild thrusts soften into excruciatingly slow, deep strokes. Our eyes lock and stay with one another as I rock into her body.

I don't know what is happening. All I know is that in this moment, nothing outside of us exists. It's just her and me wrapped up in our own little world, and all that I care about is making her moan and seeing her eyes flutter and roll to the back of her head as she cries out my name.

God, fucking has never felt as good as this. Being inside her and making her writhe beneath me has fast become an addiction I'm not ready to quit anytime soon. I plan on making my *zayka* moan and cry my name and come on my cock over and over and over again.

My balls tighten. Fuck, my body has never felt this good. This hard. This fucking drunk on another human being.

What the fuck is happening to me?

What is she doing to me?

I shift my hips to grind slowly into her, and it's her undoing. Her eyes lose focus, and her mouth parts, and a low, desperate moan falls from between her lips. Her pussy convulses around me, tight flutters that signal her release.

I slide my tongue along her damp neck as she arches it with a cry, then slam my mouth to hers and kiss her through her orgasm. And before I know it, I'm releasing into her body with a roar.

Fuck me.

Mind.

Blown.

I collapse beside her and pull her onto my chest.

She smiles against my skin and relaxes against me, and I feel her racing pulse calm and become even. "Sweet dreams, Lev," she whispers.

I press a kiss to the crown of her head and let the heady hit of dopamine soften my muscles and ease my own pounding heart.

It's probably selfish. Damn, I know it is. But I want to be the man for her. I want to love her. Protect her. Be the man she deserves. *The man she wants.*

Because I want her. I can't let her go. And any fears of becoming vulnerable because of my feelings for her pale in comparison to the fear of losing her.

I want this.

I want us.

I want forever with her.

10

BROOKE

The following day, I visit Igor in the hospital. Last night, Lev was quiet and clearly affected by seeing his lifelong friend so broken, and now, as I'm staring at the bed where Igor lays silently, I can see why. Igor is swathed in bandages, his eyes closed, and a ventilator is breathing for him.

My stomach aches. He's bandaged down to his fingers. I place mine on top of his. "I'm sorry, Igor." My voice sounds so small against the rhythmic sucking of the ventilator. "Please keep fighting."

I think about the giant man I was afraid of on that first night when Lev took me from my apartment and how, over the course of mere weeks, I somehow formed a bond with him.

I think about how sweet he and Enya looked together as they cuddled and shared a sandwich, and my heart breaks for them both.

I think about the baby growing in my belly and how one day this could be them lying in a hospital bed because their father is the pakhan, and in his world of blood and power, *happily ever afters* are in short supply.

A shiver rolls through me and I have to push the thought away. No good can come from thinking things like that.

I feel a presence behind me and swing around.

Agent Michaels.

Immediately, the hairs on the back of my neck stand up.

I turn my focus back to Igor. "How did you get past the bodyguard posted at the door?"

"It's called FBI credentials and the threat of prison time for obstructing justice."

I scoff. He doesn't want justice. He wants Lev's head on a platter so he can take it back to his bosses at the bureau and show them how tough and clever he is.

I keep my eyes on Igor as I ask, "Are you stalking *me* now?"

"Is that what Lev told you, that I stalk him?"

"He calls you his shadow," I say, then immediately regret opening my mouth.

I need to be careful around this guy. He's going to try and lure information out of me.

"I'll take that as a compliment—it means I'm doing my job right," he says, sounding pleased with himself. "Are you ready to talk to me?"

"Like I told you the other night when you blindsided me in my hospital room, I don't want to talk to you."

"It would be in your best interests, Brooke. Lev Zarkov is a dangerous man."

"What part of *I don't want to talk to you* do you not understand?" I say.

"I'm offering you a lifeline, Brooke."

I turn to look at him. "It's Miss Masters to you."

He smirks. He sees me as a challenge, and I think he likes it.

I turn away, disgusted. "What is wrong with you? Don't you have anything better to do than follow me?"

"I'm not following you. I'm following up on our conversation the other night. Thought you might have had time to reconsider turning me down."

"Do you really think you and I are going to become allies? That I will help you send Lev away for whatever fictional crimes you think he's committed?"

"He's the pakhan of the Zarkov Bratva."

"He's the CEO of a pharmaceutical company."

"You're a smart woman. You know who he is. But do you know what he is truly capable of?"

"If your plan is to try and scare me away from him—"

"You're pregnant. You've already suffered because of him. Because his rivals know about you. His fiancée. What happens when they find out you're pregnant with the heir to the Zarkov empire? I'll tell you what they'll do. They'll sniff you out and cut open your—"

I swing around to glare at him. "You finish that sentence, and I'll fucking shoot you myself."

But his eyes gleam with triumph. He's successfully sowed the seed of doubt in my mind, and he knows it.

Disgust and anger flow through me. But they are nothing compared to the fear I already feel.

He continues relentlessly. "What happens to your baby when he's done with you? When he loses his hard-on for you, and he will, because Lev Zarkov throws people away because they mean nothing to him."

"Stop."

"He won't want you anymore—"

"I said stop it!"

But he doesn't stop. He keeps throwing his grenades, and they land right in the middle of my shaky emotions.

"You will become redundant. But while you are disposable, he will never let go of his heir. What happens to you then? He won't want you, but he'll do everything in his power to keep that baby. What kind of life will it be for your child?"

His words hit exactly where he intended them to, right in the middle of the need I feel to protect this baby.

"I can protect you and the baby. Give you back a life that doesn't involve bratva bloodshed. Make sure he never touches you or your baby."

The idea of Lev not touching me or our baby is an agony I can't even fathom. I could never take this baby from him. Or leave his bed. Not now. Not ever. We've grown so close in the last few weeks. Even closer since we found out about the baby. I couldn't imagine not waking up in his secure arms.

But...

"Look at Igor," he demands. "That could easily be you lying in that bed."

I hate that he's right.

"All because you think you're in love with a man who could never love you back. You know why? Because he's a narcissistic psychopath. He doesn't do anything unless it's in the best interest of the bratva. Or his own personal gain."

Feeling my emotions get the better of me, I lean forward and gently touch Igor's fingertips to say goodbye. I need to get away from Agent Michaels.

Because he's making too much sense.

I shoot him a sharp look. "Stay away from me. I don't want your help."

I brush past him and walk to the door.

"But I want yours, Miss Masters. And I won't stop until I get it."

I hurry out of the room, desperate to make distance between me and the FBI agent.

Lev isn't home when I return to the estate. Which is good because I don't think I could hide what I am thinking from him.

That Agent Michaels made some very valid points

He's right. I don't know Lev, and I don't know what he is capable of. What happens when the shine of this baby wears off, and I become a problem to him? Only a few weeks ago, we couldn't be in the same room as one another without arguing. Now we can't be in the same room without touching each other, kissing and cuddling, fucking—no, making love—and without warning, it's got me believing in some fairytale ending.

But how can it be real? It started as a lie, and that lie has just gotten bigger and bigger and more convincing.

Feeling unsettled from seeing Igor, and out of sorts from my encounter with the FBI agent, I pace my room.

I can protect you and the baby. Give you back a life that doesn't involve bratva bloodshed.

His words haunt me.

Because what if I can't protect my baby while we're with Lev?

What if a life without the bratva is the only way to keep my baby safe?

11

BROOKE

As usual, when I wake up the next morning, Lev is gone.

But thankfully, so is the nausea and uncertainty I felt yesterday evening following my encounter with Agent Michaels.

After Lev came home last night, I didn't tell him about seeing the FBI agent at the hospital. I don't know why. Something inside pulled back from telling him. But despite not knowing about it, Lev was able to decimate the unease I felt because he was so attentive and reassuring, not to mention spectacularly creative in bed.

Now, as I lie in bed and look up at the ceiling, my body still tingles from all the things he did to me. Thanks to these damn pregnancy hormones, my libido has been ramped up a notch. It's like I can't be near Lev without putting my hands on him. He walks into a room, and I want him naked and inside me. Not that he's complaining. In fact, he seems only too happy to oblige my requests.

My phone pings with a message. I pick it up off the nightstand. It's Chloe.

> Time to put your party pants on. It's Samantha's thirtieth birthday this weekend, and either you come here, or we're coming to you to celebrate.

I sit up with a rush.

They can't come here. It would be disastrous.

But I can't keep putting them off. It's only a matter of time before they start getting suspicious. They need more than the random proof-of-life photos that I send them of the fake life that I am not living. They still think I am working for a tyrant CEO and building a new life in the city with an apartment and all the normal things someone who hasn't been abducted by the bratva would be doing. But my friends aren't fools. If they don't have some in-person time with me, then they are going to do something drastic like turn up on my doorstep.

Which would be impossible because the address for that doorstep doesn't actually exist.

I swing my legs over the side of the bed and quickly flick Chloe a message back.

> Oh, no! I was going to surprise Samantha. I am coming back to Chicago.

It's a lie, and I have no idea how I'm going to convince Lev to let me go. But I have to make this happen for everyone's sake.

Immediately, my phone begins to ring.

It's Chloe, and she's squealing down the line when I answer. "I can't believe it! Finally, we're gonna be in the same room as each other. This is going to be so much fun. It's been way too long."

Guilt washes over me because she's excited for something I'm not sure I can make happen.

"I know, I'm sorry, it's been so crazy here. But I should've made the trip back earlier."

"We understand. But we miss you. How is the evil CEO? I haven't received any requests to help you bury a body, so I'm assuming you haven't murdered him yet."

I hesitate. "Things are complicated in that department."

"Complicated? What do you mean—oh my Lord, you're boning your boss."

That's typical Chloe. Zero to a hundred in under two seconds.

"How did you come up with that idea?"

"Am I wrong?"

Again, I hesitate. "Well—"

"I knew it. You're shaking the sheets with the pharmaceutical overlord." Chloe's excitement bubbles through the phone. "Ooh, are you going to bring him with you to Chicago?"

"Maybe? It's all so new."

"Oh my God, we're going to have so much fun. I can't wait to meet him."

I smile at the thought of Lev coming to Chicago with me and hanging out with my friends. Samantha and Chloe would go bonkers over him. But Elsa would hang back and reserve her judgment until she gets to know him better. She's not easily impressed by good looks and money, and Lev will have his work cut out for him when he meets her.

And Henry, well, I think it will be love at first sight for him.

I grin, my body warm and happy when I think about my friends and seeing them again. But my smile fades because I have a huge challenge ahead, convincing Lev to let me go when his enemies have already gotten their hands on me once before. It's going to be impossible.

∼

"Absolutely one hundred percent, no fucking way!"

Lev looks at me like I've just asked the impossible of him. Which I probably have.

After hanging up with Chloe, I came looking for him and found him in his office talking with Feliks.

"I need to see my friends," I say. "They are getting antsy, Lev."

"You're not going," he replies.

I look to Feliks for help, and he gives me a look that says *good luck with that insane request.*

"I'll take bodyguards with me," I add.

Lev lifts an eyebrow. "You don't step out of this house without a bodyguard, let alone go out of state to Chicago."

"Fine, sneak me out of the city and surround me with a thousand men. But please, I need to see my friends."

I have no idea how I'm going to explain the bodyguards to my friends, but I'll figure it out later. First, I need to conquer this mountain.

Again, I look to Feliks for help, but he shrugs and holds up his hands.

I mouth, "Please help me."

He rolls his eyes and sighs, reluctantly agreeing to help.

He clears his throat and stands and approaches Lev's desk cautiously. "You know, getting Brooke out of town for a few days isn't such a crazy idea."

Lev looks at him like he's spoken to him in some ancient alien language, then leans back in his chair. "Oh, this should be good. Pray tell, why is this a good idea that she leaves?"

"There's a lot going on here, Pakhan. It might do Brooke some good to be away from the city for a while. Have some time with her friends."

I give Lev pleading eyes. "Please, I'm going crazy stuck in this house."

The hard lines of Lev's handsome face soften, and he leaves his desk to walk over to me.

"This is a very intense time for us, *zayka*. You're safer with me than without me."

"You're away from me most of the time."

He runs his hands down my arms. "Because I'm trying to end this war."

"Then let me go away. It's Samantha's birthday, and I never miss any of my friends' birthdays. I'll take bodyguards. Hell, I'll even carry one of those hand cannons that all your men seem to carry."

Feliks smiles. "I can teach her to shoot."

Lev shoots him a warning look to stay out of this. "That won't be necessary because she's not going. Let me have a moment alone with Brooke."

Once Feliks is gone, I put my hand on Lev's chest. "I need this. I won't be able to hide any of this from my friends for much longer. And my pregnancy is already beginning to show." I look down at my belly and he puts a tender hand on it, and I feel his love for this baby through the layers of clothing. "This weekend could earn us a few more weeks' grace before I have to start coming clean to my friends."

I feel bad about lying to my friends, but the longer they are left in the dark about what is happening and who Lev really is, the safer they are.

"Please," I whisper.

He looks pained. "I'm sorry, *zayka*. Now is too dangerous."

I feel my mood plummet. "I can't keep doing this. I need space, Lev. I need to breathe."

"I know, but now is the worst timing. Once I've taken care of Vlad and my uncle, you'll have all the freedom you want. We'll bring your friends here. Or you can go to them. It doesn't bring me any joy to do this, but I have to for the sake of you and the baby." His touch is gentle. "Until the threat is neutralized, you're safest here with me."

Later, I will look back on this conversation and wonder if it was the beginning of the end for us, one of the moments that led me to do the things I did in the following couple of days.

12

LEV

I stare at the reports in front of me on the desk. It's the numbers for the dementia medication trials. They look good, and I should feel happy about them, but I'm too distracted to enjoy the success. And there's one reason why.

Brooke.

She's pissed at me. For the last couple of days, she's barely spoken to me. Barely looked in my direction. And when I reach for her at night, she turns away from me.

I know her friends are important to her, and I meant it when I said it brought me no joy to keep her from visiting them. But I can't keep her safe if she isn't with me.

Her indifference is making me uneasy. She's pulling away from me, and there's not a goddamn thing I can do about it. My hands are tied because she's safest with me until Vlad is found, and I've smoked out the rat in the bratva.

"You're here early," Feliks says, waltzing into my office at ZeeMed, still wearing his suit from the night before. "Trouble in paradise?"

I send him a warning look telling him not to go there. "What are *you* doing here so early?"

"I was on my way home and remembered I left my little black book in my desk drawer." He gives me a sheepish grin. "I have another number to add to it."

His little black book is actually a phone where he keeps all the numbers and names of his hookups.

I return to looking at the reports on my desk. "Is that why you're still dressed in yesterday's clothes? Who was he or she?"

"They," he says, sinking into the chair in front of me. "There were two of them. Candi and her best friend Andrew. They were quite the pair. Hungry and rapaciously naughty. I'm going to need to rest for a couple of hours just to get my strength back." He looks at his watch. "Why are *you* here at seven o'clock in the morning?"

"There's work to do."

"There's *always* work to do."

"Well, now there is more work to do."

He sighs. "I've known you all your life, Lev, and you've never been able to lie to me. Why start now? Is it Brooke?"

"She's pissed."

"And you're surprised? You've cut her off from her life."

"A necessity."

"Maybe, but you have to expect this blowback. You could make a visit from her friends possible. Or send her out of town with security."

"It's too risky."

"Hell, I'll go with—"

"She's pregnant."

Feliks opens his mouth but shuts it again, then shakes his head, looking dazed. "Well, I'll be goddamned. Since when?"

"Since the day I met her on a plane and took her back to my apartment."

I watch him as he processes the news.

"I'm going to be an uncle?" he asks with a broad smile.

"Technically, a second cousin."

"Damn that to hell, I'm going to be this kid's Uncle Feliks." His smile grows bigger, and he claps his hands together. "And he or she is going to love me."

"I'm sure."

He sits back in the chair. "No wonder you're acting like an overprotective father right now."

"Even if Brooke weren't pregnant, I'd still be demanding this level of security."

"Of course." He grins and crosses his legs and taps his chin with his finger as he thinks.

He's about to get carried away with the idea of being Uncle Feliks—I can see it on his face. And I can't help but smile.

"Is it a boy or a girl? Wait, don't tell me. I want to be surprised. No, tell me, I've got some shopping to do, and it will come in handy knowing the sex."

"Shopping?"

"I'm cool Uncle Feliks. I'm going to spoil this kid even before it's born."

Again, I can't help but smile. "We don't know. Brooke has a scan coming up, and we might find out then."

The thought of seeing my baby on the monitor again and hearing their strong heartbeat makes me warm inside, and the uneasiness of Brooke's indifference is momentarily eased.

Feliks rises to his feet and walks around the desk to stand beside me.

"What are you doing?" I ask when he opens his arms wide.

"Come on, Cousin, this deserves a hug. Get on your feet and let me congratulate you."

Usually, I'd tell him to take two feet back, turn around, and get the fuck away from me. But after the hit of dopamine I just felt when I thought about my kid, I stand and give my cousin the hug.

He pats me hard on the back. "Does that mean I get to call you Daddy Lev?"

"Yeah, that's not happening."

He releases me from the hug. "I'm proud of you, Cousin. *A baby*. This is good news."

"We're not telling anyone yet. Not until after we've found Vlad and secured the bratva."

"Wise." He nods and taps his nose. "I'll keep quiet."

"Good." I give him a wink. "Now go away. I have a lot of work to do, and I can't afford to be disturbed."

He gives me another hard pat on the arm and then leaves the room while I return to the reports on my desk.

Several hours later, he calls me.

I mindlessly pick up the phone. "I thought I told you I didn't want to be disturbed."

"I have an update from Ibiza," he says soberly. "And I think you'll want to hear it."

13

BROOKE

To escape the house, I spend more time at the hospital because it's the only place I'm allowed to visit.

I'm still pissed at Lev about... well, *everything*. The list is too huge to repeat. But it starts with him not letting me see my friends and ends with me hating the world he's dropped me in.

Chloe was crushed that I couldn't make it back for Samantha's birthday on the weekend, and I had to live vicariously through all the photos my friends sent me of their night out.

But it wasn't the same as being there, and I can't control the resentment I feel about it. I know Lev wants to protect me and the baby. But he's taken away any sense of control I had over my life.

What kind of life will it be for your child?

I can't tell you how many times Agent Michaels' words have come back to haunt me.

Because he's right. What kind of world am I bringing this baby into?

Only two weeks ago, Vlad abducted me, beat me, and left me unconscious in an abandoned warehouse. Now I'm cocooned in this house like a precious gemstone because my baby's father has people who want to kill him.

My hand slides protectively over my belly.

"I don't know what to do," I whisper to my baby. The thought of him or her being hurt because of Lev and his bratva wars terrifies me.

I feel an overwhelming sense of responsibility. It's my job to protect this baby. But what if I don't make the right choices and something terrible happens?

I'm ripped out of my dire thoughts when Igor suddenly starts to shake on the hospital bed in front of me, his entire body stiff as if he's being electrocuted. Alarms go off.

He's having a seizure.

A doctor and two nurses rush in. One of them ushers me to the door. "You can't be here."

I see Igor jerking around on the bed, and I'm terrified for him.

"Is he going to be okay?" I beg the nurse.

"He's very unwell. You need to leave. *Now.*"

I back out of the room, my heart pounding.

Is Igor going to die?

Tears form in my eyes, and suddenly, all the fear and uncertainty of the last few days catches up with me, and I start to cry.

From the doorway, I watch the scene unfolding. Nurses and doctors struggle to stop him from convulsing.

Terrified he's going to die, I start walking backward to put some space between me and what is happening in that hospital room until I hit a solid form behind me. I spin around and come face to face with Agent Michaels.

Before I can stop him, he puts his arm around me and pulls me in for a hug. And I'm so busy sobbing it takes me a moment before I realize what is happening, but when I do, I push him away.

"I don't need you to do that," I say, taking a step back.

He nods. "Understood."

I swipe away my tears. "What are you doing here?"

"The same as you. I've come to see how Igor is."

"Since when do you care about him?"

"Since he might become a witness when he wakes up."

I glare at him. "Igor would never betray Lev."

He looks over my shoulder, and I turn to see what he's looking at. Igor is still shaking on the bed, but the medical staff are able to bring his convulsions under control, and he settles.

"This can't be fun for him," Agent Michaels says. "I wonder how he'll feel about things when he wakes up."

I snap back to look at him. "You're a piece of work. Preying on people when they're feeling emotionally low."

"I'm just doing my job, Brooke."

"I told you, it's Miss Masters to you."

He smiles, but despite his movie star good looks, I can see what really lies behind his white smile and Californian tan. He's a dog with a bone, and he's going to do whatever it takes to keep it.

"Goodbye, Agent Michaels."

I brush past him, but he takes me by the arm.

"Todd Bastik is up for parole," he says.

A sudden wave of emotion surges through me, and all I can do is stare at him.

Ten years ago, Todd Bastik spent the day drinking and getting high on meth before climbing into his truck and driving to the local liquor store for another bottle of rum. Already out on bail for vehicular manslaughter, he was so drunk and high he could barely walk. He only got a mile down the road before he collided head-on into the car my father was driving. My mom was in the passenger seat, and I was in the backseat listening to Nine Inch Nails on Spotify.

Within seconds, my family was wiped out because Todd Bastik was a selfish asshole who didn't care about anyone or anything other than himself and a damn bottle of rum.

Agent Michaels' eyes gleam. "He's been a model prisoner. He'll probably get it."

More tears well in my eyes. "But his sentence was for eighteen years."

Agent Michaels holds his hands out like it's out of his control. "He's been a good boy."

I can't stop my chin from quivering because damn Todd Bastik and damn any parole board that lets him free.

Ten years.

Is that all my parents' lives were worth?

"But I can stop it from happening," Agent Michaels says. "I know three of the parole board members very well. My word will go a long way. You want to keep your parents' killer in prison, I can make that happen. All I need from you in return is the right information about Lev."

I think of my mom in her last moments. How frightened she was because she didn't want to die. How her fingers went loose in my hand, and her body settled heavily against mine as she died in my arms.

How I couldn't save her.

"Tell me what I need to make sure Lev pays for his crimes, and I will assure you Todd Bastik will continue to pay for his."

Is this my chance to make it up to my mom for not being able to save her that night?

To ensure her killer remains behind bars like he deserves?

I look at Agent Michaels. He's offering me a way out of this big pile of crazy I've been dropped into, and he'll keep that monster Todd Bastik from getting parole.

My hand slides to my stomach.

But I won't betray Lev.

He's the father of my baby.

Yet it's getting harder and harder to stay in a world where I would even have to consider it.

14

LEV

I get home at nightfall. It's been hours since Feliks called to tell me the update from Ibiza.

Upstairs, I find Brooke in our bedroom, curled up on the bed, reading.

She looks up when I walk in, and I can feel the tension in the room. But it's not the same frostiness I've felt since denying her a visit with her friends. This is something new. *Something is off.*

"Is everything alright?" I ask. "Is the baby okay?"

Putting down the book, she climbs off the bed and walks over to me. "The baby is fine. I'm fine. Well, kind of."

"What happened?"

"Todd Bastik, the driver who killed my mom and dad, is up for parole, and Agent Michaels thinks he will get it."

Fuck. I know all about Todd Bastik and his pathetic history. About the lives he ended. I read all about him in the file Feliks compiled for me when I was looking into Wilson and Brooke.

"Didn't he get eighteen years in prison?"

"Yes, but apparently, that means very little when you've been a model prisoner." Her eyebrows are drawn in, and I can see the pain in her eyes. "And before you offer, no, I don't want him dead. I want him to live out the rest of his sorry life in prison."

I can't help but smile. My little hell bunny. She knows I would have him taken care of in prison with one word.

She lifts her lashes and hits me with her big brown eyes. "Can you do anything to keep him in prison?"

While ensuring Todd's demise in prison would be as easy as a phone call, attempting to sway a parole board is something else altogether. It would require weeks of compiling information on people to use against them. Using someone's darkest secret against them so they will do your bidding is most effective in these kinds of situations. But that takes time, and we don't have it.

Although, it doesn't mean I can't have someone look into it for her.

"I can't promise anything on short notice, *zayka*, but I will do what I can." I run my hands down her arms. "Killing him would be easier."

"Yes, for him. His miserable life would be over, and I don't want the easy way out for him. I want him to live the rest of his sorry life out in prison where he isn't able to hurt anyone else."

I nod, but I'm preoccupied because I know the news of Todd Bastik's release isn't the only upsetting news she's going to receive. Because I'm about to deliver some more.

And she picks up on it. "What's wrong?"

I'm all for getting straight to the point in moments like these, so I rip off the Band-Aid quickly.

"Wilson is dead."

For a moment, she doesn't move. She just stands there, her big brown eyes wide with surprise as my words settle over her.

Then her shoulders drop, and her eyes narrow. "How?"

Going by the look on her face she thinks it was me.

"I didn't do it."

"Then how did he die?"

There is a sharpness in her tone.

She doesn't trust me.

After everything we've been through, she still doesn't trust me.

"He was found in his hotel room. They suspect a drug overdose. They won't know until the autopsy and toxicology confirm it."

She blows out a deep breath and walks slowly to the bed and sits down on the edge. "What about the flash drive?"

"One of our associates on the west coast has already secured the flash drive."

Her eyes dart to mine. "When?"

"When it was clear Wilson wasn't come back with it. I put things in place to retrieve it from the safety deposit box."

It wasn't easy. And it cost me a lot of money. But the flash drive is gone. I personally saw to it myself.

Brooke nods, but she's preoccupied by her thoughts.

"I didn't do this," I reaffirm. Back when she agreed to pretend to be my fiancée, I vowed that I wouldn't hurt him. And now, more than ever, I need her to know I wouldn't break my word to her.

But the way she looks at me tells me she is wary, and damn that stings.

"Did you still have eyes on Wilson in Ibiza?" she asks.

"Yes."

"Do they know what happened?"

"Only that he and a couple of young women retired to his villa for the night. The next day, one of the women called for an ambulance, but it was too late."

She nods, clearly speechless. She did all of this for him. Ended up here, for him. And now he's dead.

I cross the room and crouch in front of her so we're at eye level. "Are you okay?"

She scoffs and shakes her head. "I can't believe it."

"I know it's a shock."

She bites her lip. "What's wrong with me?"

"What do you mean?"

"I should probably be crying, right?"

"People process grief in different ways."

"But that's it. I don't feel any grief."

"You don't feel sad about it?"

She shakes her head. "No, Wilson lost my empathy the moment he left me to the wolves. That's you, by the way. You're the big mean hairy wolf."

I smile, but I know her humor is masking the enormity of what has happened. I take her hand and gently run my thumb over the soft skin. "I'm going to run you a bath. Let me take care of you tonight."

She nods, and I press a kiss into her lips before I lead her into the bathroom and run her a bath. While she soaks in the warm, bubbly water that smells like sandalwood and rainforest, I order dinner for us both to be brought to the room, then strip off my clothes and join her in the giant tub.

Wrapping my arms around her, I hold her against my chest and feel the tension ease in my shoulders.

"Am I a bad person?" she asks in the soft candlelight.

"You're one of the kindest people I know," I say truthfully. "I don't know anyone who would do what you did for him."

"There was little choice in the matter."

I weave our wet fingers together and hold her hand up so her diamond engagement ring winks in the dim light. "Whatever decisions were made that night were the best decisions of my life."

When she doesn't reply, I feel the distance between us deepen. She's different from how she was only a few days ago. But I don't press it, hoping I am reading too much into it.

After we dry off, we make love in the soft light of our bedroom. We take it slow and gentle, enjoying the slow build-up. I feel utterly consumed by her as I kiss and lick and stroke deep into her. But despite her moans and the way she cries my name when she comes, it still feels like something has broken.

I don't know what we are. I don't know how any of this is going to work. But whatever we are, in the last couple of days Brooke has become disconnected from me.

You kept her from her friends, and she's still pissed.

But it feels more than that. And as I wrap my arms around her and listen to her fall asleep, I have to fight off the dark whispers in my head that tell me I am going to lose her and force myself to get some sleep.

But my sleep is short-lived.

Just before midnight, my phone rings. It's Feliks. He knows the news I was delivering to Brooke tonight, so he wouldn't be calling unless it was important.

"Did you find Vlad?" I ask.

"No, but we found the next best thing."

I know exactly who he is talking about.

"Good. Bring him to me."

15

BROOKE

I don't know what wakes me up, but sometime in the early hours of the morning, I realize Lev isn't lying beside me. According to the clock, it's 3:21.

Overcome with a sudden craving for pistachio ice cream, I leave the bedroom and make my way through the maze of passageways and down the staircase toward the kitchen.

The mansion is quiet and still.

Except...

Standing in the massive kitchen, devouring ice cream from the tub, I notice lights moving about outside. My curiosity piqued, I move to the window to see where they're coming from. The window looks out over the immaculate lawn and across to another wing of the mansion, which has been under construction since I arrived here, and it's there through the shadows I can see lights moving around.

I know there is nothing to be afraid of. Lev has made it clear that this place is heavily patrolled, so it's probably some of his men. But I decide to check it out anyway. I'm wide awake and feel up for some middle-of-the-night exploration.

Taking my ice cream and spoon, I set off through the mansion. Access to the forbidden wing is by two tall doors at the far end of the passageway. Usually, they're locked, but tonight they're slightly ajar.

Go back to your room, that little voice tells me.

Which, of course, I ignore.

Instead, I creep through the parted doors and step into a world so different from what lies behind me. Instead of fine furnishings and muralled walls gilded in gold, the room I'm standing in is nothing but a shell full of construction material and scaffolding up to the ceiling. Plastic hangs from one part of the ceiling, separating the rest of the room from whatever restoration is taking place behind it.

It's the middle of the night, so no such work is taking place. But I can hear voices.

Holding my breath, I inch closer and peer around the plastic to see what is on the other side.

I see Lev standing with several of his men, looking down at something on the ground. As I get closer, I can see there is a man on his knees in front of him, and he is speaking rapidly. Swearing and yelling, bits of spittle flying out of his mouth.

I recognize him. He's the orderly who attacked me at the hospital the night of the explosion.

Finally, Lev lifts his gun and shoots the man in the forehead.

I gasp and quickly slap my hand over my mouth.

But it's too late.

Lev turns his head, and our eyes lock for a long, painful moment, and I realize I am looking into the eyes of a killer.

My body freezes as I glance at the dead man slumped on the floor in front of him.

Get out.

Get out.

Get out.

I begin to back out of there, unable to take my eyes off the dead man at Lev's feet.

"Brooke." Lev says my name, and it snaps me into action.

I turn and run.

I run all the way back to the main wing but eventually stop when Lev's voice reaches me. It's so guttural and sharp, I come to a halt at the base of the staircase. "I said stop."

I swing back to him. He is walking along the corridor toward me, every step purposeful, every stride confident. He looks so self-assured and collected. Not at all like he just killed a man.

"You shouldn't have been there," he says.

I swallow thickly. "I heard voices."

He eyes the spoon and ice cream in my hand. "So you thought you'd check it out and take care of whatever it was with ice cream and a spoon?"

"I had a craving." I look up at him. "He was the man who attacked me at the hospital."

"Yes. He was also the man who built and planted the bomb."

I think back to the car explosion. The bright burst of light and the shockwave that rattled the glass in the windows.

Goosebumps creep along my arms.

"Who was he?" I ask, remembering the violent fear I felt that night.

"A bomb maker for hire. Don't mourn him, *zayka*. His particular skillset has cost hundreds of people their lives."

"But you killed him so easily."

"Yes. Because he deserved it."

I knew Lev was capable of dark things. But actually seeing him shoot a man dead scares me.

He offers me his hand, and because I don't know what to do, I leave my ice cream and spoon on the step and take it and let him lead me into his office.

I'm not afraid of him. Or what he could do to me. I already know he would never do anything to harm me or his baby. But this sudden intimate insight into his world has rattled me.

He moves to his desk, but I linger at the door, as if moving any deeper into the room will pull me deeper into a world I don't belong.

"Come," he says. "I want to show you something."

I cautiously approach the desk where he is spreading photos across the polished wood.

They are crime scene photos of what were once buildings and cars, even a private jet.

He points to a photo of a building with the side blown out and the interior spilling onto the street. In the center of the picture is a lone high heel lying on its side.

"Seventy-two people died. Most of them women. But he got the required destruction he was hired to create, so he considered this a win." He points to another photo of what was once a boat. "In this case, the target wasn't even on the boat, but an entire family of innocent people died." He points to the plane. "And in this one, nineteen people never made it home." The muscle in his jaw ticks as his dark eyes roam over the photos. "All of this destruction. All of these dead people. It all happened because of that man out there."

Looking at the photos, I feel sick, and I wrap my arms around my waist. My baby isn't even born yet, and I feel the need to hold it in my arms and protect it from the horrors I see in the pictures spread out before me.

Lev lays another photo out. It's of his car. "He wanted to kill me, Brooke. And afterward, he tried harming you and our baby. I wanted to know who hired him."

"Did you find out who?" I can't take my eyes off the burnout wreckage. I could've lost Lev so easily that night.

"Yes."

I lift my gaze to him. "Who was it?"

"Vlad fucking Bhyzova."

16

LEV

Dammit.

Watching me put a bullet in that *mudak's* head was the last thing I wanted Brooke to see. Especially when I know something between us has fractured. Witnessing a man's murder has taken us another step back. I can see it in her beautiful face. The wariness. The fear. She's wondering if I could ever turn that violence on her.

I brush my thumb over her cheek. "I will do whatever I have to when it comes to your safety and that of the bratva."

I need to reassure her that she will never know that side of me. That I will not only protect her from my enemies but from that side of me too.

But it doesn't change the facts. Brooke has seen something she can never unsee.

It was an error in my judgment, bringing him to my home. But I'm fucking exhausted. The plan was to get the information out of him, then dispose of him as quickly and efficiently as possible.

I walk with Brooke back to our room and sink down on the bed beside her. With our heads resting on the pillows, we face each other.

"I know what you saw tonight has frightened you, *zayka*. But tonight, I saved hundreds of people from becoming his victims."

"I know. But you did it so easily. You didn't hesitate taking his life."

"Because I know what he is capable of and what he's already done." I reach over and brush stray strands of her hair from her face. "He put his hands on you and threatened you and our baby. What do you expect me to do?"

"I get it. I mean, when I think about our baby, I know I will do whatever it takes to protect them too," she says softly. "But seeing it…"

"You need to understand that when I find Vlad, I will do the same thing. Take his life easily. Except it won't be quick like a bullet to the head. It will be far more brutal because it has to be done. This is my world, *zayka*."

I see the wariness in her eyes. No, not wariness. *Fear*. And it damn near kills me to see it.

But for this to work—for her to live in my world—she needs to hear this.

"War is coming, and more blood will be shed. To keep you and the bratva safe, I have to act swiftly, and sometimes that is bloody."

She looks away.

"I'm scared," she whispers.

I trace soft fingertips over her cheek and along her jaw, and she brings her gaze back to me. "You have nothing to fear. I will always keep you safe."

I pull her into my chest and hold her as she falls asleep. But sleep eludes me. Even with my sweet bratva lullaby sleeping soundly in my arms.

Because tonight, Brooke caught a glimpse of the true darkness of my world and the kind of things I have to do, and now my instincts tell me we are entering troubled waters.

Because what will she do now that she knows what I'm truly capable of?

17

BROOKE

The strange sensation sits heavy in my chest as I fall asleep in his arms, and it's waiting for me when I wake up in them the following morning. It lingers in my chest as I watch Lev walk into the bedroom fresh from his shower, with a towel wrapped around his narrow hips, his glorious six-pack on display, and his golden skin dripping wet with shower water. It coils tightly in my chest as he dresses for work in another expensive suit, and it burrows deeper as he kisses me goodbye, his hair still damp from his morning shower.

When I hear his car, I climb out of bed and watch him drive down the long driveway, pass through the gates of the Zarkov estate, and disappear out of view.

War is coming, he says.

More blood will be shed, he says.

I think about the man on his knees, begging for his life. I think about the bullet Lev put in his forehead.

How many more men on their knees will there be?

Feeling numb, my hand glides over my stomach. Perhaps I could navigate this new life if it were just me. But now I have someone else to consider.

There is only one choice I have left.

Run.

18

LEV

My first indication that something is wrong is when she doesn't answer my phone call.

When the next three attempts also go unanswered, I feel a strange sensation begin to form in the pit of my gut.

I tell myself she's probably left her phone on charge and has forgotten about it. But my instincts have never let me down before, and right now, they're letting me know something is wrong.

I call Enya. If there is one person in my household who will know where Brooke is, it is her. But Enya is at the hospital and hasn't seen her. So I call Maria, my housekeeper, and ask her to look for Brooke in her room. While I wait for her call me back, I leave the office, climb into my car, and head for home with a skid of tires and a gut-wrenching knowledge that something is wrong.

During the drive, I call my head of security. There is an impenetrable wall of security around my home. There is no way anyone could make it in without any of my men seeing them. And if Brooke had decided to leave she would need to leave in a car.

"She definitely hasn't taken a vehicle, Pakhan," says Pierce, my head of security. "And no one without clearance has been inside the estate walls."

"You're certain?"

"I'd stake my life on it, sir."

His life might very well be at stake if anything has happened to Brooke.

"Look for her," I demand before hanging up.

I try Brooke again, but again, frustratingly there is no answer.

Maria calls me back. She sounds worried, which does nothing but pour fuel on the growing unease in my gut.

"I'm sorry, Pakhan. But I couldn't find her anywhere."

~

She's gone.

I storm through our bedroom and into the bathroom, but she's not there.

She's not fucking anywhere.

I run a frustrated hand through my hair. My heart is racing, but it's nothing compared to the rising panic in my gut.

Has someone taken her?

I'm about to leave the room when I see an envelope leaning up against the lamp on the bedside table. I rip it open to find a note inside.

If you love your baby, you'll let us go. Your world is not our world. I'm sorry.

Panic turns to relief.

Relief turns to anger.

She's left me.

She's taken my baby and run.

Inside the envelope is the credit card I gave her and her engagement ring. Seeing the ring is like a hammer hitting me in the chest.

I crumple the paper in my hand as my chest tightens with the knowledge that she's run away from me.

She's scared.

But I thought we were on the same page. That despite the horrors of my world, we had become something more than the deal to keep Wilson alive. More than a fake arrangement. I thought we had built something real. But clearly, I was wrong, and fuck, getting slammed in the balls would hurt less than this.

My phone rings. It's Feliks.

I don't give him a chance to speak as I answer. "Brooke's gone. Do you know where she is?"

"No. *Fuck*. Are you sure?"

I tell him about the note.

"How did she leave without any of the guards seeing her?"

"Good fucking question," I growl just as my head of security walks in.

"Alright, I'll do some digging and see if I can find out anything."

I hang up and glare at Pierce. "I want a list of names of everyone who has come in and out of the estate today."

"Already got it. Other than my security team, there was only one visitor to the estate today."

"Who?"

"Joe, the food delivery guy."

19

BROOKE

I'm either a genius or the world's biggest fool, I think to myself as I ride in the back of Joe's delivery truck. Either way, this is what I have to do.

I can't have my baby growing up in a world where you can be kidnapped and beaten to prove a point to your rival in crime.

Another thing I can't do is think about what it will do to Lev when he finds out I'm gone. I'm taking his baby, and I know it will hurt him, and I feel that pain already in my chest when I think about it. But I can't let that distract me from what I have to do to protect this baby. It's not about me or Lev anymore.

The truck hits a pothole, and my bones rattle with the vibration. It takes me back to the night of the explosion, and I shiver. I'm cold, and my bones are stiff from sitting in this cramped position for the last twenty minutes.

The plan is to sneak out of the truck when Joe stops for his next delivery and find somewhere safe to stay the night. I'll admit this isn't the best thought-out plan. Time was of the essence when I decided to flee.

Finally, after what feels like the bumpiest, longest ride in the history of driving, Joe pulls up and opens the back door. I hold my breath and squeeze my eyes shut, hoping he doesn't see me hiding behind a stack of boxes toward the rear of the truck.

Fortunately, he pulls out a tray of bread and then leaves, and I see my chance to finally sneak out.

Outside, it takes my eyes a moment to adjust to the late afternoon light. It's going to be dark soon.

You need to find somewhere safe to sleep.

We're parked out in the front of a strip mall. Across the intersection is a gas station, and next to it is a motel.

I dash across the road and disappear inside the motel. An older lady with a kind face is behind the reception counter and looks me up and down when I walk in. She looks for my luggage but doesn't say anything when she realizes I don't have anything. Going by the dated furnishings and original carpet from the eighties, I think discretion is this motel's selling point.

"It's twenty-five dollars for the night, sweetheart," she says.

I don't have any cash or a card, but luckily, I have my Apple wallet on my phone.

But then I remember, Lev will be able to trace that.

Damn it. How am I going to do this without him finding me?

I call Henry, who is currently staying in my apartment back in Chicago, and he answers on the second ring. "You know, I could get used to living here. Do you know you're in the delivery area for the best Chinese food in the city?"

"That's great, Henry, but I need your help."

Hearing the tone in my voice, he's immediately concerned. "Why do you sound so panicked? Is everything okay?"

"Yes, I'm fine and safe, but promise me you won't freak out when I tell you that I need a motel room for the night and that I need someone other than me to pay for it."

He pauses, then says, "And that someone else is me, I take it."

"Yes."

"Are you okay? Wait—" His concern turns to wicked suspicion. "Is this for some kind of tryst? A little afternoon delight between you and a mysterious stranger?"

I hold back telling him I'm done with mysterious strangers.

"No," I say emphatically.

"Does he have a wife? A girlfriend? Is that why neither of you can use your own credit card?"

"There is no one else here but me."

He goes quiet for a beat.

Then I hear the concern in his voice again. "What's going on, baby doll? Should I be worried about you? Oh my God, is someone forcing you to make this call? Say *the kitty litter is in the pantry* if you want me to call the police."

I can't help but chuckle. Henry is an avid armchair detective. He watches so much Crime Channel he could probably commit the perfect murder.

But then the memory of Lev shooting the man on his knees in front of him flashes through my mind, and a cold shiver rolls through me. In my old life, murder was a foreign concept. In this new one, it's a fucking regular occurrence.

"I'm fine, I promise, but I'll explain it all to you later."

He doesn't sound happy, but he doesn't push me. "Okay, let me get my credit card."

After Henry gives the lady behind the counter his card details, she slides a key across to me. My room is at the far end of the motel and only accessible via the parking lot.

As I make my way along the path, I see a lady waiting in the doorway next to mine. A man pulls up in a car in front of her room and walks over.

"Hey, baby, you Candy Kane?"

"Yeah, sugar. You my three o'clock?"

"That's me, baby, Mr. Three O'clock." He chuckles.

"Well, best you get your cute ass inside, baby."

They disappear behind a closed door just as I pass by, and I hear laughter and then Candy Kane saying, "Oh, you're a keen one, aren't you, baby? Come here, big boy, and give that thing to mama."

I unlock the door to my room and am immediately hit with the odor of stale carpet, musty window furnishings, and Lysol.

Closing the door behind me, I sit down on the bed and stare out at the neon vacancy sign outside my room.

This is my life now.

This is how it has to be.

I look at the business card in my hand.

Agent Garrett Michaels.

Pulling my phone out of my jeans pocket, I ignore my protesting heart and dial his number.

20

BROOKE

"Okay, I need to know what the hell is going on," Henry says on the other end of the phone.

After hanging up from my conversation with Agent Michaels just a few seconds ago, it's nice to hear Henry's friendly voice. Even if it is demanding and dripping with concern.

"Let me start by saying you have nothing to worry about," I lie.

Because let's face it, right now, I have a bratva pakhan looking for me, and who knows what he will do if he finds me.

"When people say not to worry, it usually means the opposite," Henry replies.

"Maybe, but Henry, this is really important, and I want you to listen to me carefully. I need you to pack a bag and go and stay in a hotel for a couple of nights."

"What, why?" He sounds worried. "You're scaring me, Brooke. You need to tell me what is happening right now."

I gnaw on my lip. I've gone over how this conversation might go a hundred times in my head, and each time, it ends with Henry panicking and me hating myself for putting my friend in possible danger. It doesn't take a genius to predict Lev will send someone to my apartment, and I don't want them finding Henry when they get there.

I let out a rough breath and then tell Henry the well-crafted story I made up for my friends. How I met Lev on the plane on my way to my *honeymoon for one* and the amazing night we shared together in New York City. How he turned out to be my boss, and that, at first, we tried to keep things professional, but one thing led to another, and we ended up embarking on a red-hot love affair. But now that love affair has burned out, and I need space from the powerful CEO as I try to figure out what I do next.

"There's a lot for me to unpack there, and you better believe we're going to circle back to each point, especially how you never told me… your closest male friend … that you had a one-night stand in New York City. Does Elsa know?" He gasps when I don't answer immediately. "You told her and not me? I'm hurt, but I love you, and you're letting me stay in your apartment, so I will forgive you and move on. But just so you know, I'm terribly hurt and scarred." He lets out a dramatic exhale. "Does Elsa know what's been happening while you've been in New York City?"

"No, and don't tell her. She just had a baby, and I absolutely don't want her involved. She has enough on her hands. She doesn't need to worry about me."

"What about Sam and Chloe?" I hesitate answering, and again he gasps dramatically. "They know about the hot CEO boyfriend?"

"Only that I was seeing him. But they don't know we've broken up."

Henry sighs and then asks, "How does any of this require me to stay at a hotel for the next few days?"

"Because Lev will come looking for me."

"His name is Lev? Mmmm, he sounds sexy—is he Russian?"

"Not the point here, Henry."

"Right, of course. Why will he come looking for you?"

"Because he's not as into breaking up as I am."

"Riiight." He pauses. "Are you in danger? Should I be calling the police for you—"

"No, nothing like that." I downplay it, and I hate that I'm keeping so many things out of the conversation. But it's for his own benefit. I can't have Henry do something stupid like getting the police involved. Hell, I don't want my friends involved in any of this, and I have to protect them from the fallout, no matter what.

"Why do I feel like you're not telling me everything?"

"Because you watch too much Crime Channel." Outside, I see a set of headlights pull up. I tense up but relax when I see the driver disappear into Candy Kane's room. "Please, will you do this for me?"

"Fine, I always wanted to stay at the Museum Hotel, so I might as well stay there."

"Good, my treat." I try to keep my tone lighthearted, but it's hard when I'm worried for my friend.

"Did I say Museum Hotel? I meant The St. Regis," he says, swapping the four-star hotel for the famous five-star hotel.

I chuckle. "Nice try."

He sighs. "Is it really a necessity? I mean, what are the chances he's going to come banging on my—"

Through the phone, I hear a knock on his door, and a bolt of panic zips down my spine like lightning.

"Henry—"

"It's okay, it's just the Chinese takeaway I ordered," he says, answering the door and accepting his takeaway from the delivery guy. The door closes again. "You sound so panicked."

"Because I don't want you to get caught in the middle of this."

"I'm not even really sure what *this* is. You say he's not dangerous. He's just a rich prick who doesn't want to let you go. I'll just tell him to fuck off. But, you know, nicely, because I don't want to break the guy's heart any more than you're already breaking it."

I have a feeling it would take a lot to break Lev Zarkov's heart, and I don't think my leaving him would even come close.

But what if it's not Lev who shows up but one of his men, and they get heavy-handed with Henry? I would die if Henry got hurt.

No, Lev will go looking for me himself.

Because I'm carrying the heir.

"Please, can you just go stay somewhere for a couple of days until I figure out my next move?"

"Your next move should be coming home. I'll stay with you, and if Mr. CEO turns up, I'll protect you."

Yeah, I can't see that happening.

Lev could mow down Henry with a blistering look. There are not too many people he couldn't.

Henry's voice lights up with excitement. "It will be fun living together for a while. Lots of homemade dinners and cocktail nights, how does that sound?"

It sounds perfect. But impossible.

Because he doesn't know the truth.

I know if I told Henry everything, he would be advising me to do something completely different. Go to the police, he would say. And that's why I can't fill him in. Because going to the police wouldn't work out very well for me. Knowing Lev, he's probably tight with everyone in the Chicago PD.

So, for now, I'm going to sit on the truth and hopefully keep Henry and Elsa and the girls safe.

I sigh, resigned to doing this myself.

"Let me sleep on it, and I'll call you tomorrow."

21

BROOKE

After I hang up from Henry, I lie on the bed and stare at the movie playing on the TV. But I'm not paying attention. All I can think of is the pain of what I am doing. Not just to me.

But to Lev as well.

I wasn't going to eat, but Henry ordered me some tacos and had them delivered to the motel room. Despite not feeling hungry, I force them down because I know I have to fuel my body for the baby at least.

Somehow, after rechecking the door and window locks, I manage to fall asleep.

But just before midnight, I wake up and immediately feel the empty space beside me, and it feels cold and dark and lonely.

He's not there. And he'll never be there again.

I stare up at the ceiling.

Missing Lev is midnight poison. The ache. The longing. The knowing I can never go back. I know I am doing the right thing. But the guilt of what I am about to do keeps me awake. And the empty space beside me is a cruel, cold reminder that I am doing it to him.

I know he doesn't love me.

But he already loves this baby.

And he is never going to see either of us again.

22

LEV

It's late as I sit at my desk and stare at the crumpled note before me.

The only sound comes from the flames in the fireplace. It's not cold, but I find the sound of flames licking and snapping soothing, so I indulged and lit one despite the warm temperatures outside. But whatever comfort I thought they would bring tonight, they are failing. Same with the three vodkas I've downed. Nothing can ease the ache I feel. The feeling of loss. *The crushing ache I feel because she left.*

I pick up the diamond engagement ring from the desk and hold it up. In the light of the flames, the diamond blazes with a thousand different golds and reds. She just left it behind like it meant nothing.

I remain calm. Only because inside, my pain and anger are simmering and building and waiting for more information before reacting.

But it's getting harder to hold them back.

She left.

The thought is on repeat, and I loathe the tight stab I feel in my gut every time I think of it.

I twist the diamond ring around my finger, hypnotized by the spangles of light as I sink deeper and deeper into my thoughts.

Why didn't she talk to me about her fears?

Why didn't I tell her how I feel about her?

Would she have stayed?

A knock on my door pulls me out of my trance, but I keep twisting the engagement ring around my pinkie finger as Feliks walks in carrying a folder.

"Courtesy of my contact at the surveillance division of the police department."

He places the folder in front of me on the desk, and I open it.

Street cam photos.

The first one is of Joe's truck parked out the front of a restaurant. It's taken from a distance, so the image is grainy and blurred, but it's easy to make out Brooke climbing out the back. The next is of her standing at an intersection, waiting for the lights to change. The third is from a different camera facing a different part of the intersection, and it shows Brooke walking toward the Merriweather Motel.

"Do we have eyes on the motel?"

"There was no record of a Brooke Masters checking in."

"But?"

"But an Ivy Aimes checked in, and the room was paid over the phone by one Henry Aimes."

"Her friend back in Chicago."

I remember the name from the dossier I had Feliks compile about her all those months ago. Back when I was lying to myself that my instant interest in her was solely because I was hunting her fiancé and not because I was slowly becoming obsessed with her.

Feliks brings up an image on his phone and shows me. It's Brooke at the reception counter, signing in. No doubt Feliks had one of our tech wizards hack into the motel CCTV once he'd found the street cam footage.

"They didn't want ID?" I ask, unable to take my eyes off the photo of her.

"Let's just say the clientele turnover is high. Hourly in some cases."

"Do you have a room number?"

"Yes, I have put a couple of men in the parking lot. They'll keep watch until we get there. Want me to drive?"

"I'm not going."

Feliks lifts his brow. "You don't want to see her."

She left.

"Not yet."

"You want the men to bring her in?"

"No one goes near her," I growl, taking Feliks by surprise.

He looks confused. "You want to leave her there?"

No, I want her here with me in my bed with this ring on her finger.

"Yes, that's exactly what I'm going to do."

Feliks clearly doesn't agree with my plan but knows better than to argue. "You're going to let her leave?"

Not while there is breath in these lungs.

"No, let me sit on it. Tell the men I want a pair of eyes on her at all times. If she leaves, they follow. And I want to know who she talks to and where she goes."

Feliks nods. "I'll make sure that happens."

He turns to leave but stops before he reaches the door and turns around. But he hesitates before opening his mouth.

"What?" I snap, my mood darkening with every twist of the ring around my pinkie finger.

"She's just scared, you know."

But I don't reply. I know she's scared. She should be. This world I've pulled her into is full of danger at every turn. But she should know I can protect her. Will protect her.

And she will.

Very soon when I make my next move.

Feliks leaves. He knows I'm better off left alone when I'm like this.

The reason I'm not going after Brooke is because she ran away from me, which means she doesn't want to be with me.

And until I figure out what this pain in my chest really means whenever I think about it, then I'm not making a move until I'm sure it's the right one.

Because there is more at stake here than I could ever have imagined.

23

BROOKE

The next morning, I meet Agent Michaels at a diner down the road from the motel.

He's already waiting in one of the booths by the window when I arrive. Dressed in his black suit and tie, he looks out of place amongst the interstate truckers and early morning construction workers pouring in and out of the diner for a pre-work coffee and bagel.

I slide into the booth opposite him and order a coffee from the waitress when she stops by the table.

"I must say, I was surprised to get your call," Agent Michaels says once the waitress leaves. "I was starting to think we couldn't be friends."

I feel sick, and I don't know if it's the morning sickness or the fact that despite his earlier charm and good looks, there is something very icky about Agent Michaels. A wave of nausea rises and falls in my stomach, and I make a mental note of where the restrooms are because I have a feeling I'm going to need them.

"Let's make no mistake about it, we are not friends," I say, noticing how his bright blue eyes narrow slightly but how his white smile remains intact. "But I am here as a courtesy to you."

His brow lifts. "You are? You got something you want to tell me?"

"I broke up with Lev."

This time, his whole body shifts with surprise. "When?"

"Yesterday. I told him it was over and walked out."

"And he let you?"

"Yes."

Again, his eyes narrow slightly. "Just like that."

"He didn't have a choice."

"He let you walk out and take his future heir with him?"

"I'm having an abortion," I lie.

He scoffs. He knows I'm lying. "And he didn't even try to stop you. Well, I'll be damned."

Those blue eyes burn across the table at me, waiting for me to crack.

But I don't. I stare right back.

Two nights ago, I saw Lev murder a man right in front of me. I think I'm beyond intimidation from this guy. Especially when I've got a much bigger fish in the pond after me than this guppy.

"I'm leaving town," I say.

Agent Michaels stares at me with a well-practiced, scrutinizing gaze, and it makes me wonder how many people he's made talk just by staring at them this way. But then, without warning, his demeanor suddenly changes. His face softens. "Let me help you. Like I said, we can keep you safe. Tell me what I need to know in order to put this guy behind bars."

I shake my head. "I'm not telling you anything."

"You're afraid, but you don't need to be. We can protect you."

I laugh coldly. "You can't protect me from him. He's smarter than you, and his reach is even broader than you could imagine. He'd find me. Besides, that's not why I'm here."

His face hardens. "Then why are you here?"

"I'm here to give you an official statement."

He eyes me suspiciously but then pulls out his phone and places it on the table in front of me. He brings up a recording app and hits a bright red button to record.

"This is Agent Garrett Michaels, and I'm sitting with Brooke Masters, who has requested to make an official statement." He nods to me. "Please state your name."

"My name is Brooke Rachael Masters."

"And this is a statement you are making of your own accord?"

"Yes."

"And what would you like to state for the record?"

"That I am no longer Lev Zarkov's fiancée. We broke up, and I've decided to move on with my life. Lev was nothing but a gentleman during our time together, and I have no knowledge of any criminal behavior that you claim he orchestrates. Lev is the CEO of ZeeMed and a champion of those suffering from dementia. If you need proof of any supposed crimes that he has committed, then you will need to find someone else to back them up because I certainly can't."

Agent Michaels has gone still and quiet. It's like I've just dropped a bomb on the table.

"That's your statement?"

"Yes."

He stops the recording. "You fucking little bitch." He says the words quietly but with a razor-sharp edge on every syllable. "You're protecting him?"

"No, this is me protecting my baby." I glower back at him. No point pretending I'm having an abortion anymore.

His eyes glow across at me, his high cheekbones pronounced in the early morning light streaming in through the window. He looks like he's about to erupt. "I'll make sure you go down as an accomplice."

"I have nothing to do with Lev. I'm done with him, and I'm done with you. Stay away from me and my baby. And if you have any sense, you will stay away from Lev. He's a good man, despite what you think."

Agent Michaels suddenly grabs my wrists on the table. "You listen to me, and you listen to me good, you fucking cunt. I'm going to make sure that piece of shit goes down, with or without your help. I don't care what I have to do, or what I have to fucking embellish, I'm going to destroy everything about him, everything he cares about, and if I have to start with you, then I fucking will."

I try to remain calm. "Let me go."

But he's only getting started.

"I've worked too hard and too long on this, and no one is going to stop me from taking him down. Not him. Not you. Not the fucking law. I will do whatever it takes. Say whatever it takes. Lie through my fucking teeth, if that's what it takes."

My eyes widen. "You'll make it up?"

I don't know why I'm surprised. Michaels is clearly obsessed and desperate. Not to mention, *unhinged*.

His lips pull back in a sneer. "My whole life I've watched men like him get what they want, and when they want it. And if it doesn't come easy to them, they just take it. The job. The opportunity. The homecoming queen."

"Is that what this is about? You didn't get the pretty girl in high school?"

He squeezes my wrists tighter, making me wince.

"You want to have your baby in prison? Because if you walk away I will make sure that happens. And you know what else I'll do? I'll make sure you never see it. Now tell me what the fuck I want to know, or so help me God, that bastard baby in your womb will never know either of its parents."

I wrench my wrists free.

"Do you get off on trying to intimidate pregnant woman, asshole?" I snap, rubbing my wrists. "Stay away from me or I will make a formal complaint."

With my pulse pounding in my ears, I slide out of the booth and start to walk away.

He calls out. "He'll go down, Brooke. And I'll make sure it hurts you."

But I keep walking away and disappear out of the diner.

24

LEV

"You look like you haven't slept," Feliks says, walking into my study.

It's early afternoon, and I'm running on adrenaline and caffeine. My fourth cup of coffee sits half-finished in front of me.

"I got a couple of hours." It's a lie. I got nothing but a night spent tossing and turning in my bed while sleep eluded me. "Any update from your men posted outside her motel room?"

He holds up the folder in his hand, and by his expression, I know it's not going to be good news.

"You need to see these," he says, placing the file on my desk.

"What are they?"

"Seems your shadow has been making contact with Brooke more times than you thought."

I let out a rough breath.

My shadow. Of course, he's involved in this somehow.

I open the file. The first series of security camera photos are of Brooke and Agent Michaels talking at the hospital. The second series of photos are of the two of them again, clearly on a different day, and it looks like they're at the hospital again. But Michaels has his arm around Brooke, and it looks like she's burying her face into his shoulder.

They appear very cozy.

My hands curl into fists on the desk. I squeeze them so tight my fingernails pinch into my skin, and my knuckles glow white.

She's in his fucking arms.

"What the fuck is this?" I growl.

"It's what it looks like, Lev. Brooke was meeting with Agent Michaels at the hospital."

Inside me, the possessive monster wakes up and roars.

Feliks looks empathetic. "I don't want to say it—"

"Then don't," I snarl, hating the thought that Brooke might've betrayed me to Michaels, feeding him information about me and the bratva.

"I don't like it any more than you do. I love Brooke. But look at the photos, Lev. Is it such a stretch to think that she exchanged information so he would help her escape?"

"She stowed away in the back of a food truck and had her friend pay for a motel room. If Michaels was helping her, then he's doing a shit job." I look at the photos, hating the churning in my gut.

"There's more."

My eyes dart from the photo to Feliks. "What?"

He sorts through the photos until he finds a set taken this morning. It's of Brooke and Agent Michaels talking in a diner.

My gut twists painfully.

Feliks removes a letter from his suit pocket. "And this also came through this late this morning."

It's a notification of a denied parole application. I'm about to ask what it has to do with any of this when I see the name on the application. Todd Bastik. The man who was put away for Brooke's parents' deaths. He was eligible for parole. But today, the board denied it.

And now Brooke is missing.

"Reach out to our contact in the justice department. Ask him what swayed the parole board's decision to deny that fucker his freedom."

"I already did. Apparently, a certain FBI agent wormed his way into their ears. Well, according to talk around the water cooler."

I feel Feliks hesitate.

"What aren't you telling me?" I demand.

"Our contact also confirmed someone is definitely talking to the FBI. Someone in our circle. I'm sorry, Cousin, but it can only be her."

"More water cooler gossip?"

"Perhaps, but sometimes it's the most reliable source." He sighs, not enjoying this. "All roads seem to be pointing to Brooke being the FBI's informant."

His words might as well be a punch to my face.

Every muscle in my body tightens with the pain of her disloyalty.

"If someone is talking, why haven't I heard about it earlier?" I growl.

"Because it only just happened."

"It might not be her. I already suspected we have a rat."

"Not a rat talking to the feds. A rat talking to Vlad. This is different. Besides, Brooke met with him today. Our contact said this new witness has only come on board recently. He doesn't have access to exact details, like dates and names. Only that it's recent. You don't believe in coincidences, and neither do I."

He's right. I don't. Where there is smoke, there is usually fucking fire.

A heavy weight lodges itself deep in my chest.

"Can this contact probe deeper? Find out a name?"

"He said the details for this case are shrouded in extra security. You know how much Michaels wants to take you down. He's not leaving anything to chance. He's made it so only certain levels of security clearance can gain access to the information."

"What about that other contact you had? The woman you used to date. Doesn't she have high clearance in the FBI?"

"Olivia?" He looks sheepish. "She's currently unavailable."

Meaning his dick has somehow burned that bridge.

I sit back in my chair, my shoulders tight with tension. "It might not have been Brooke. I want to start looking for a rat in the bratva."

Feliks frowns. "You know how much I like Brooke. I don't want it to be her. But even you can't deny that those photos and Todd Bastik's parole denial make her look guilty."

"Perhaps, but we need to be vigilant and not get tunnel vision with this."

"I agree, and I hope I'm wrong about her. But we also can't afford to let your feelings to get in the way of this."

I glower at him. It sounds awfully like he is questioning my judgement. If it was anyone else but him I would wipe his face off his head with my bare hands.

I grit my teeth. "I don't let any emotion cloud my judgement."

"No but you've never had feelings for someone like you do with Brooke."

"She's carrying my child."

"And that's the extent of your feelings for her?"

"No, it wasn't." I look at the photos and Todd Bastik's denied parole notification and I feel the betrayal right down to my bones. "But it is now."

I feel a beast wake up inside of me. One born to protect me from putting blind faith in someone because I've contracted some kind of feelings for them.

And right now its reminding me exactly why Brooke *would* do this.

I stormed into her life and relentlessly pursued her.

I broke into her apartment and pointed a gun at the man she had once loved enough to marry.

I ripped her from her safe life—the one where she didn't have to worry about car bombs and assassination attempts—and forced her to live with me in my world.

All because of one fateful day when I caught a glimpse of her and decided I wanted her.

All because of one moment that gave birth to some sick obsession inside me that needed to make her mine.

Since then, she's been a pawn in my fantasy. I've taken her freedom from her and backed her into so many corners she got confused enough to fall into bed with me again and again.

And in my bed, I pulled her further away from the light and deeper into the darkness, where she sank deeper and deeper with me.

Now, Agent Michaels has pulled her away just far enough for her to see the light again, where she can have her old life back. One that includes her friends and a world that doesn't cause her the same pain as mine does.

So the question isn't *why* she would do this.

It's why the fuck wouldn't she?

25

LEV

After Feliks leaves, I stare at the photos of Brooke and Agent Michaels.

I think back to the day she was meant to marry Wilson. How I had driven past her apartment and saw her exit the limousine in her wedding dress. How it felt like I had been struck by lightning when she glanced over her shoulder, and I saw her beautiful face for the very first time.

I became weak in that moment. Obsessed by just one glance.

And since then I've made a series of mistakes, starting with letting her into my bed, and ending with letting her into my heart.

I even got carried away by the idea of loving her and raising a family.

Like I could live a normal life. Be a normal man.

But I won't make that same mistake again.

If I could banish every trace of her from my life, I would. But she's pregnant with my baby, and whether I like it or not, that ties us together for an undetermined amount of time.

I will make sure she is looked after. Protected. She can live here with our child while I reside in the penthouse. Our contact will be limited and only ever have to do with the baby.

But I'll be damned if I let her back into my bed, let alone anywhere near my fucking heart.

From this point forward, Brooke Masters is the woman carrying my child and nothing more.

And I'll make certain she understands it.

26

BROOKE

I barely sleep. And again, in the middle of the night, I wake up missing Lev. My body physically aching for him.

But I feel better after having it out with Agent Michaels. Hopefully, now he's got the point and will leave me the fuck alone.

I toss and turn for most of the night, only falling asleep when I cuddle the pillow and pretend it's Lev's warm body I'm curling into. So I'm feeling groggy and only half awake when there's a pounding on my door.

My nerves fizzle and pop. Has Lev found me? My heart hopes so, but my head prays he hasn't.

Today, I leave New York City for good. I will call Henry and ask him to send me some money so I can catch a bus home. At least, surrounded by friends, I will be able to figure something out.

But I don't have to call Henry, because one look out the window and I see him standing on the doorstep.

When I open the door, I throw my arms around him, suddenly realizing how alone I've felt for the past couple of days.

"Hey, baby girl," he says soothingly. "It's okay. I'm here."

I start to cry. "Don't worry, these aren't tears are sadness. They're tears of happiness." I swipe them away with the back of my hand. "What are you doing here?" I ask once we're inside the motel room.

But the moment I close the door behind us, I have to run to the bathroom and throw up. Morning sickness, my ass. More like around-the-clock sickness.

When I come back out, Henry is sitting on my bed, looking suspicious.

"Are you sick?" he asks.

"No," I reply, elusively.

He crosses one leg over the other and gives me a very serious look. "I'm here to take you home. But before we go anywhere, I need to know everything, baby girl. I know you're holding back on me. If I'm to help you, I need to know everything."

I can't tell Henry everything. It will put his life in danger.

But I will tell him everything I can.

"If my boyfriend finds me, he won't let me leave."

"Why?"

"Because I'm pregnant."

27

BROOKE

Ten minutes later, we sit down in one of the booths at the diner across the road.

"Pregnant?" Henry is still in shock. "How did that happen?"

"How do you think?"

"Wait, is it Wilson's or Mr. Mysterious'?"

"It's Lev's."

"So it's early days."

"Not as early as you'd expect. I got pregnant the night I met him."

Henry's eyebrow goes up. "You didn't use any protection?"

"Let's just say it was all very surreal, and I took a lot of risks. But the point is, now I'm having his baby."

"Yet you're hiding from him." He frowns. "He didn't hurt you, did he?"

"No, Lev would never hurt me." The words leave my lips without thought. Because I know Lev wouldn't hurt me. I mean, he might break my heart if I let him. But he would never physically harm me.

"Then what's the problem? Is he a dick?"

"No, he's very charming."

"He's a selfish lover?"

"No, he gives me multiples before he takes his own."

"Ooh, I like this guy. Wait, he doesn't have bad personal hygiene, does he?"

"No, he's very manscaped in a rugged, primal way."

"Small dick?"

"Big."

"Chews with his mouth open?"

"No." I chuckle.

"Oh boy, is he married?"

"Nope."

"Then why did you run away?"

I glance around the diner and then lean in. "He's Russian mafia."

His eyebrow shoots up. "He's in a bratva?"

"He *is* the bratva. He's the pakhan. The boss."

That's when Henry does something I completely do not see coming.

He throws his head back and laughs.

"Why are you laughing?" I ask, confused.

Henry shakes his head, seemingly not seeing the danger of me having the pakhan of a bratva hunting me down at this very second.

"You had a one-night stand with a pakhan." He chuckles as he shakes his head, and I'm confused because I kind of thought he would freak out, not find it amusing and exciting. "I dated a Russian mobster once."

"You did?"

"Hottest sex of my life. Had the biggest cock on him, and the fucker knew how to use it." He fans himself. "Could deep throat too. Best head of my life, actually."

"Then what happened?"

"He was always breaking dates because he had to, I don't know, go kill people or something."

"Henry!" I exclaim.

He chuckles. "I'm kidding, I mean, maybe."

Our waitress brings over coffee and takes our food order. Pancakes for me. Waffles for Henry.

I wait for her to leave before asking, "Why did you never mention your Russian mafia boyfriend?"

"Because I knew you'd freak out and tell me to end it... and well, the sex was too damn good."

I get it.

How many times had I wanted to call my friends and confide in them about Lev, but I didn't because I was worried they'd snap me out of my delicious delusions that my involvement with Lev would have a happy ending.

If I had, maybe I wouldn't be in this mess.

But would you have even listened to them?

I gnaw the inside of my mouth. "I've seen what his world looks like, and I don't know if I want to be a part of it."

Henry's face grows serious. "Has he ever been violent?"

I think of the man on his knees begging for his life.

"Not toward me. I don't think he could ever hurt me. Even in the short time I've known him, I know he lives by certain principles, and violence toward women... well, he'd consider that uncouth." I shake my head. "He's only ever been protective and giving, and not just in bed. He's offered me a life that most people could only ever dream about."

"It doesn't sound like you want to leave him."

"I do."

"You don't speak like you do."

"Then how do I speak?"

"Like you're crazy in love with him."

"That's not true," I say, busying myself with the cup of coffee in front of me.

The waitress brings us our meals, and I'm suddenly ravenous and dig into the pancakes like I haven't seen food for months.

"So come back to Chicago. I'm already staying at your apartment. I can protect you."

I look at my gorgeous friend, hating that I have involved him. He could never protect me from Lev. But I don't tell him that. Instead, I go on enjoying my pancakes and the fact that Henry is here because even though he is no match for Lev, he makes me feel safer than if I were alone.

After devouring his waffles, Henry licks his fingers. "Come on, let's go back to your motel and call the airline so we can get you home to Chicago." He gives me a comforting smile. "Everything will work out, you'll see."

I don't share his optimism, and he can tell.

On the table, he slides his hand over mine. "I've got you, kid."

I clasp my fingers around his. "Thank you for coming here. It really does help."

He grins. "You know me, I'm always up for an adventure."

We leave the diner, cross the intersection to the motel, and make our way through the parking lot.

The moment I see the black Escalade out the front of my motel room, my body does two opposing things.

One, my adrenal glands send a surge of adrenaline through me because I know Lev's found me, and I don't know what that means for me.

And two, I feel a second surge follow the first, but this one is a big wave of excitement crashing into me. *Because Lev's found me. And there is some fucked up part of me that still aches to see him.*

I glance around, but I can't see him.

What do I do?

My fight or flight kicks in, and I decide flight is the better option. Because I don't want Henry involved in this.

"Henry," I whisper. "We have to get out of here."

I turn to look for an escape route that doesn't involve going past my motel room, but the moment I turn, I collide with a rock-hard chest standing right behind me. I look up and see a pair of familiar dark eyes and a tight jaw.

"Hello, Miss Masters." His voice is cold and hard. "Going somewhere?"

28

LEV

Feliks and I follow Henry and Brooke into the little motel room and close the door behind us.

"What the hell is going on?" Henry demands.

"Henry, this is Lev," Brooke explains, not meeting my eyes.

"And I'm Feliks," Feliks jumps in, immediately shaking Henry's hand.

Henry's eyes light up. "Well, hello…"

Feliks gives him one of his flirtatious grins, and the two make eyes at each other like we're all here on a fucking Tinder date.

I clear my throat.

Both men turn to look in my direction, and Feliks straightens like the soldier he's supposed to be.

"How did you find me?" Brooke asks.

"You left in a refrigerated delivery truck. Common sense says you'd get off at the next stop. Not a very smart move hiding out in a motel across the road from where Joe's next stop was."

"Well, forgive me for being an amateur at running from the mafia."

"Bratva," I remind her.

She continues to shoot bullets at me from her eyes.

The motel room is a shithole.

This was better than being with me?

"You're coming home with me," I say, unable to control the edge in my tone.

"No, I'm not," she bites back.

"And not if I can help it," Henry says, taking a step forward.

I shift my gaze to him. He's clearly intimidated, but I have a feeling he'd throw himself in front of Brooke to stop me from getting to her.

I like this guy.

He knows who we are, and he's still got the balls to stand up to me. I admire his need to protect her. Even if it is futile. Because stopping me from taking Brooke home with me will be like trying to stop a volcanic eruption. *Impossible.* I have layers and layers of destruction boiling inside me, ready to blow, and the anger ready to detonate it. But I respect his willingness to try. He cares about her. Not because he wants to fuck her but because he genuinely loves her, and I appreciate that.

I give Feliks a knowing look, and he understands immediately. I want time alone with Brooke.

He turns to Henry. "Perhaps you and I should step outside and let these two talk."

Henry shoots Brooke a look. *What should I do here?*

"That's very good advice you should listen to," I say to him.

Brooke nods, and Henry lets Feliks guide him toward the door.

"You smoke?" Feliks asks.

"Only after sex," Henry replies absentmindedly as he watches Brooke and me with a concerned look on his face.

Feliks smirks and gives him a wink. "Let's have a cigarette first and then see how we go, shall we?"

Once they're gone and it's just me and my little runaway, I gesture for her to sit.

Which she refuses, of course.

"I'm fine right here."

I send her a warning look. "Sit down."

She gives me a filthy look but sits on the edge of the bed anyway. "If it means we can get this over and done with quickly."

"Oh, that's not going to happen."

I admit it's hard to look at her because I'm barely containing the anger inside.

She fucking left me.

And since she scurried away like a frightened little mouse from me, I've had a million arguments with her in my head about it, and she hasn't won a single one of them.

Now that I'm here looking at her for the first time since I found out she sold me out to the feds, I'm surprised by the pain twisting in my gut.

"You and I have a few things to discuss," I say.

"Fine, but let's get this over with. Say what you're going to say."

She looks tired, and the part of me that wants to look after her tells me I should go easy on her. Forget that she just ran without talking to me. Forget that she put not just herself in danger but our baby as well. Forget that I'm dying to take her in my arms and hold her because I'm fucking relieved we found her before any of my enemies did.

But the other part of me that felt the pain of her leaving me is bigger and angrier, and right now, he's in control, and he's determined to make sure she knows it.

"I know what you did," I say.

Which puts her off guard because her brow pulls in with confusion. "Yeah, it's kind of obvious that you know I ran away from you when you're standing in front of me in my motel room."

My little runaway has developed an attitude, and I don't know what I want to do first. Punish her or kiss her.

"I'm talking about your breakfast date with Agent Michaels."

Her back straightens, and I can see the surprise written all over her face.

"You know about that?"

"I know about every time you spoke with him."

"*Every* time? What are you talking about?"

I bring up the images on my phone and hold it out so she can see the screen. "At the hospital." I flick my finger across the screen to bring up the different photos, stopping at the one where he has his arm around her. *Fuck, that one still fucking hurts to look at.* "That's my favorite. You two look quite cozy."

She sits up straighter and hits me with big, beautiful, angry eyes. "What the hell are you suggesting?"

"I'm not suggesting anything. I'm just laying out the facts in front of you and asking you to explain them." I stop on the next image of them at the diner yesterday. "Tell me, did you sell your soul to the FBI for the price of a cup of coffee?"

I see the moment when her anger turns from a slow burn into a simmering rage. Her nostrils flare, only slightly, but enough for me to know that I've hit some kind of button.

"You think I am involved with Agent Michaels somehow?"

"You can't deny you look… chummy. Did he offer you protection? Did he tell you to sneak into the back of Joe's truck so he could get you away from me?"

"No, I did that all on my own, and don't you dare take any of this out on Joe. He had no idea I was in the back of his truck, and he had no cause to, so don't you do anything to him."

"Look at you, always quick to save everyone else around you. Everyone except me, of course." I hate how my words come out with more emotion than I intended. I'm not used to dealing with this much emotion running through me, which is another reason to keep Brooke as far away from me as possible. My feelings for her made me weak, and they're still making me weak if I can't keep them out of my tone.

But I can't stop. It's like my mouth has a mind of its own.

"What's the plan? Is he going to meet you back here and whisk you away to your new life? Is he going to step in and help you raise my baby?"

The idea of any other man being a father figure to my kid makes my body shake with unchecked rage.

Brooke's eyes widen with shock, and I feel like I've hit the nail on the head, and my fists tighten to hard balls at my sides.

"I have nothing to do with him. I told him to leave me alone." Her eyes narrow. "And I don't need anyone to help me raise my baby, do you understand? I am capable of doing that on my own."

"Well, that's not your choice now, is it? That baby is going to have you and me to raise it. And no one, not even an ambitious *pizda* like Agent Michaels, is going to stop that from happening."

She stands up. "I told you, I have nothing to do with him. I told him to leave me alone."

I can't help the scoff that erupts out of me. "You expect me to believe that?"

"If you don't know me by now, and if my word means so little to you, then we have nothing left to talk about."

I disagree. "We have a lot to talk about. And it's not gonna happen in this shit hole of the motel. You and Henry are coming back with me."

"Like hell we are."

"You speak as if you have a choice. But let me be clear… you don't."

"What are you gonna do, kidnap me again?"

"Yes, Miss Masters, that is precisely what I am going to do."

29

BROOKE

I should probably be afraid of what Lev is going to do once he gets me back to his estate. But I'm too pissed off to be scared. In fact, I am furious. He thinks I ratted him out to the feds. After everything I've done. After every word I've kept. After everything we've been through. He dares to question *my* integrity.

He doesn't look at me. Just stares straight ahead like he's a robot. Back straight. Shoulders tense. Jaw tight. Dark energy radiating off him like antimatter.

Whereas, I can barely sit still in the back of the car for all the angry energy tearing through my body.

I read somewhere once that babies can feel what their mothers are feeling inside the womb. So I tell myself to calm down. But being calm is too big a mountain to climb right now. Not when the asshole responsible for making me feel this way is sitting right next to me as still and as incommunicative as an Easter Island statue.

My anger bubbles up inside me, and I decide it's better out than in, so I turn to the man who has become the bane of my existence and tell him exactly what I think of him.

"You have some nerve accusing me of going to the feds."

"It's not an accusation." He doesn't look at me. Just keeps looking straight ahead. "I have the pictures to prove you did."

"I admit I met with him. But only to tell him to leave me alone."

"You really expect me to believe that?"

"Yes."

Finally, he turns his head to look at me. His eyes are cold and dark. "Are you telling me he didn't offer to speak to the parole board to keep Todd Bastik in prison?"

"He offered, but I turned him down."

"You'll have to be a little bit more convincing than that. Bastik was denied parole. Thanks to your little friend in the FBI."

That detail manages to break through my red-hot anger, and I'm grateful that Todd is still behind bars. Even if it makes me look guilty. But I don't give a damn if Lev believes me or not. The fact that he's even questioning my word when all I've ever done is stand by it, well, fuck you very much, Mr. Pakhan.

"That had nothing to do with my conversation with Agent Michaels."

He looks away. His jaw is sharp. The muscle in his cheek is twitching. He's more than angry at me. He's furious. And not just about me meeting with the FBI. He's angry at me for leaving.

I cross my arms and turn away to look out the window.

What did he expect me to do?

Play happy families when the world around us was burning down?

∽

"Are you okay?" Henry asks over his shoulder as we pull up to the gates of the Zarkov Estate.

He and Feliks have been talking quietly during the entire drive. While Mr. Robot and I sat in icy cold silence as we both stared out the window.

"I'm fine," I say to Henry, and he smiles.

He and Feliks are getting along well. Which is a good sign that no one is going to get murdered here tonight.

Well, except Lev. Because I've already done that a thousand times in my head since we left the motel room. Nope, wait, I started murdering him in the motel room right about the time he accused me of ratting him out to Agent Michaels. Who, might I add, Lev has also decided I want as my new baby daddy.

Because Lev is an asshole.

The gates open, and we drive toward the grand house at the end of the long driveway.

Henry whistles in awe. "My God, who are you people?"

When we stop, I attack the car door handle until Feliks disconnects the child lock, and I climb out, slamming the door behind me.

Lev follows and slams his door louder before storming up the front steps behind me.

"Where the hell do you think you're going?" he fumes.

"To my room."

"Oh no, you don't. You're coming with me." He takes my arm. "We haven't finished talking."

I yank my arm free. "If you think I'm going anywhere with you only to hear you accuse me of being anything but a good sport about any of this, then you're as delusional as you are insane."

"And if you think you have a choice about any of this, then you're just as delusional."

"As if I've ever had any choice about any of this," I yell.

"Then this shouldn't be a surprise," he yells back.

Feliks interrupts. "Um, Pakhan…"

Lev and I both turn and snap in unison, "*What?*"

Feliks and Henry are standing at the bottom of the stairs, watching us.

Feliks tips his head toward Henry. "Where should I put our guest for the evening? I mean, I'm happy to entertain him so you two can keep yelling at each other some more."

Lev glares at his cousin. "Keep an eye on him. He doesn't leave until I've sorted things out with Miss Masters."

Henry doesn't look concerned. And why would he? I can see it on his face—he thinks this is some kind of sexy argument between two people who are hot for each other. In fact, he looks like he's having the time of his life. Especially when he hooks his arm through Feliks' and they walk up the stairs and disappear inside together.

I see my chance to get away from the angry pakhan and storm inside behind them, but Lev is faster and catches up with me. He takes my arm again, drags me down the long palatial corridor to his office, and slams the big, heavy door shut behind us.

I shake him off and step away. "Stop manhandling me, asshole."

"Oh, *I'm* the asshole?"

"Yes."

"Remind me again, who ran away without a word and then dined with the FBI?"

I roll my eyes because I'm not prepared to go around in circles anymore. I point a finger at him and press it into his chest. "That's not me being an asshole, that's me protecting my baby."

"*Our baby*," he seethes. He takes a step closer, forcing my back to the wall behind me. "And no one can protect you and our baby like I can. If you think you can outrun my enemies, you're wrong. You think you can outrun me… then you really don't know what a tenacious fuck I can be. If you run, I will find you."

Heat flares in his eyes, and I don't doubt what he says.

I suck in a breath to steady my nerves as well as my aching nipples and the insane throbbing that's taken up between my thighs. Because while my head is angry and ready for murder, apparently, my body is ready for something else entirely. Being this close to him is doing crazy things to every part of me. He's too much. The heat coming off of him. The intense dark looks on his handsome face. And don't get me started on how enticing his scent is. It reminds me of safety and orgasms. And unfortunately, my body remembers all too well how he gives them.

He towers over me, but his face is only inches from mine. *Close enough to kiss.*

I push my palm into his chest. I need space. Air. *A psychiatrist.*

Even now, as he takes my choice from me by bringing me back here, my body aches for his touch and his need. Not this maniac who is all hard lines and gruff words.

So when he slams his lips to mine, I respond by grabbing him by the collar and kissing him back. Hard.

His kiss is like fire, his lips hot and demanding, his tongue strong and commanding. He takes my jaw in his palms and kisses me harder, sending an overwhelming need sweeping through my body.

I reach around and cup his ass, groaning when I feel his erection.

I want this.

I need this.

The throbbing between my legs pounds relentlessly, and my hips seek out his, searching for the rigid outline of his cock because I need friction, goddammit.

He shoves my hands above my head and holds them there with one hand while the other hooks under my leg and lifts it high so he can step in between. He presses the rigid outline of his erection into me, and I almost come from the contact alone.

I gasp in his mouth and grind against him, and he groans, and it's a primal rumble that only fans the flame.

His lips find my shoulder. My neck. And travel up to the soft spot below my ear.

My breath hitches.

He grinds against me, and I begin to pant.

His hands roam my body, setting it ablaze.

His lips find my mouth again, and his kiss is fierce. His hand slides between us and rips open my jeans, popping the button and breaking the zip. He slips his fingers beneath my panties, and I tremble when they brush past my clit and slide inside me.

"You like getting me worked up until I fuck you with my fingers against the wall." He groans into my shoulder. "You're so damn wet."

I'm not just wet. I'm sopping wet.

His fingers rub my clit in maddening circles before sliding inside me, then come back around to torture my clit again.

I'm a hot mess against the wall.

I hate him.

I really do.

But right now, I want to come more than I want to hate him.

And why shouldn't I?

He owes me this much.

I moan. "*Oh...*"

He rubs my clit faster. Thrusts his fingers deeper. Grinds his palm harder. And I unravel like a ribbon against the wall, clinging to him as days of pent-up emotion burst out of me, and I cry out his name as wave after wave streams through me, turning my bones to liquid.

I sag against the wall and struggle for breath.

I need him inside me.

I reach for his zipper, but he stops me. Our eyes meet, and I don't see lust in them. I see only darkness.

His fingers circle my wrist. "No," he growls.

I'm still high on a heady mix of afterglow and an eager anticipation for more, but the tone in his voice cuts through the blissful haze. It's cold and hard. *Emotionless.*

I frown. "I don't understand."

The muscle in his jaw ticks. "This is the last time we touch. I will make sure nothing like this happens again."

Suddenly cold and clammy, I pull my hand free from his grasp. "Then what was that?"

Did he just give me some kind of revenge orgasm?

"That was goodbye." He couldn't sound or look more cold if he tried. "You and I are done, Miss Masters."

Hurt soars through me.

And I feel stupid.

Stupid for letting him touch me.

Stupid for not wanting it to stop.

He did this to hurt me.

No, he did this as payback for me leaving.

He'll say it's because of my meeting with the FBI, but I don't think that's what upsets him the most. I think my leaving gave him the bullet, and he just fired the gun.

He's trying to hurt me because I hurt him.

No, to hurt him, he'd have to have feelings.

I shove him in the chest. "You jerk."

I hope he's proud of himself.

But there isn't a look of amusement or delight on his face. No, his face is dark and stormy like he's too angry to enjoy this.

I move away from him before he can see my tears. Because I refuse to give this man any more of my tears. *Any more of anything.*

Feeling petulant and unhospitable, I cross my arms and set my jaw. "So this is how it's going to be? I'm your prisoner in this big cold house, and you're just going to ignore me?"

The look he gives me is ice cold. A stark contrast to the heated lust mere minutes ago.

"Call it what you will. But from now on, Miss Masters, you are nothing more to me than the woman carrying my baby."

30

LEV

I watch Brooke make for the door. "Where do you think you're going?"

"Away from you, or haven't you filled your quota for being an asshole yet?"

I take a seat behind my desk. "Don't tempt me. I'm sure I could think of a few more things to say."

She huffs out a breath. "If you must know, I'm going anywhere you're not."

"Just a reminder that there is no point running. My men know to detain you."

"Do they know I'm pregnant too?" she snaps. "Or have they been instructed to stop me no holds barred?"

That surprises me. As if I'd let my men lay a finger on her. I would cut off the head and hands of any soldier who dared to touch her in that way.

"How about you don't try to find out."

I don't look at her as I busy myself with some paperwork on my desk. But I feel the resentment burning off her in waves.

Good.

I want her to hate me.

Maybe then I won't fuck up like I just did and give into my own needs just so I can feel her.

Or taste her sweet lips.

Or make her face fill with carnal need.

Or hear her moans as she comes.

I will have to be stronger.

"From this point forward, you will be issued a new credit card to cover anything you or the baby needs. Spend it on what you will. There is no limit."

"I run away, and you give me another credit card... as punishment?"

"It will limit our need for contact," I say coldly.

Her expression tightens. "And after the baby is born?"

"You and the child will reside here. While I will reside at the penthouse in Manhattan."

"You've got this all figured out," she says in a soft voice.

And I can hear the hurt in it, and I hate how weak it makes me feel.

I don't reply.

"Is that all you have to say about the matter?" she asks, a harsher edge to her tone.

"Yes, you are dismissed."

I don't look at her, but I feel her blazing glare.

She storms out, and once she's gone, I have to adjust my aching cock. I'm so hard it's painful, and I just gave myself a giant case of blue balls. But I bite back the urge to make myself come because right now, I don't even trust myself to fuck my own hand without thinking about her. Because I know, without a doubt, it will be her I am thinking about as I stand on the precipice of coming, and it will be her I think of when I fall.

No, moving forward I won't even let myself fantasize about her.

Instead, I pour myself a vodka and throw it back.

Then another.

And another.

You are nothing more to me than the woman carrying my baby.

They were cruel words. But necessary. Because if she hates me, she'll steer clear of me.

But seeing her big eyes fill with hurt cut me deeper than it should, and I hate the regret that lingers in my chest.

Another good reason to limit our encounters. To avoid feeling like this again.

So the plan is simple. In future, I won't look at her. I won't talk to her. I won't do anything that puts me in close proximity to her. Because right now, I wouldn't be able to do any of those things without revealing just how much pain I am in.

If what just happened against the wall is anything to go by, one wrong word from her and my feelings would bubble over, and I wouldn't be able to hold myself back from snapping at her, and she wouldn't be able to stop her natural instinct to fight back.

We would argue.

Then, we would let our emotions get the better of us.

And before the argument was over, I would do something really stupid like take her into my arms again and kiss her lips till they're raw, and then take her into my bed where I could never, ever let go of her again.

So no. I will stay out of her way and force myself to keep our interactions to a minimum.

I pour another vodka because I want to forget about her. About us.

Because touching her, kissing her, and making her come have forced me to admit what I have been lying to myself about for months.

I have fallen in love with her.

Plain and fucking simple.

And I fell hard.

But that was before she ran off and had breakfast with the FBI.

Now that love is dying a slow, painful death, and I can feel the heavy weight of its death rattle in my chest. It doesn't want to leave, but the darkness in me is slowly squeezing the life from it.

And I'm going to let it die.

31

BROOKE

I'm too angry to go to my room. I'll just end up pacing the floor. I need to talk this through, and not with the detached psychopath currently sitting behind his desk in his monster's lair. I'm too hurt to even be in the same room as him.

For him to use my own weakness for him against me... well, he's just evil.

But then, what did I expect from a cold-blooded monster?

Walking through the colossal mansion, I decide I need to talk this out. I need some female energy. But I know Enya will be with Igor at the hospital, and Maria will be retiring for the evening to watch her shows in her bedroom. And, of course, I can't call any of the girls, so I go looking for Henry even though I have a feeling he might be busy with Feliks.

I find Henry and Feliks in the kitchen, laughing as they drink vodka.

When I walk in, Henry's laughter fades. "Everything okay?"

"He's a jerk. No, he's a giant asshole of a jerk." I flop down at the table beside Henry. "And I hate him."

"The pakhan has a lot on his plate at the moment," Feliks says.

"That may be the case, but I think him being a grumpy ass is his default setting."

"He has a lot of responsibility on his shoulders."

"Don't we all? And we don't go around kidnapping people off the street."

"You are here for your protection and of the baby," Feliks reminds me. "You're carrying his heir, Brooke. You have to expect he is angry that you left. Especially after everything that happened."

"What happened?" Henry asks.

"One of Lev's enemies kidnapped Brooke and put her in the hospital to prove a point to Lev."

Henry turns his head sharply. "You conveniently left that bit out."

"I'm sorry. I wanted to ease you into the whole *I'm involved with the bratva* thing."

Unfortunately, Feliks doesn't know when to keep his mouth shut. "And then with the car bomb—"

I cringe, knowing Henry isn't going to take it well.

He stands so fast it almost gives me whiplash. "Car bomb? What the actual hell, Brooke?"

"It's okay," I say, taking his wrist and guiding him back down to the chair. "I wasn't hurt. I wasn't even there."

Because technically, I was in the building next door.

"Best you tell me everything," he says. "And this time, don't leave anything out."

I tell him what happened. About Victor dying and Igor being in the hospital.

About the attack in the hospital.

About the war on Vlad.

"And in the middle of all of this, Brooke flees," Feliks adds.

I narrow my eyes at him. *Traitor.*

Henry rests his elbows on the table and runs his hands through his hair, exhaling roughly as he tries to process everything I just told him.

Suddenly, he straightens. "This is really happening."

I glance over to Feliks, who looks relaxed and at ease as if he's watching a PG movie and not two friends discussing car bombs and kidnapping.

I guess after a while, this life must get desensitizing.

I give him a pointed look. "Don't forget the bit where I sold Lev out to the feds."

"You have to admit, Todd Bastik being denied parole immediately after you met with Agent Michaels looks suspicious."

"Yes, it does. But things aren't always how they look. I met with him so I could tell him to back off. He's been pestering me for weeks, and I'm over it. So I decided to let him know that he was wasting his time trying to get anything out of me."

Feliks' bright blue eyes study me for a moment. He is usually easy-natured, but the way he is looking at me right now, I can see he's looking for holes in my story or little signs in my body language that tell him I'm lying. I can see how intimidating he would be to those who cross his path in the dark underworld that he and Lev reign so royally in.

But then he smiles, and he's an entirely different person.

And I know which version I prefer.

"Give him time," he says. "He's hurt because you left."

"Only because he sees it as me getting the better of him."

"You're not giving him much credit. He was concerned about you and the baby. I know you don't want to hear it, but your life changed the moment you became pregnant. You're carrying the Zarkov heir, so you must understand his need and want to protect you both."

"I do understand that bit. But does he have to be such a cold-hearted dick?"

"I don't deny he can be cold, but that is just a front. You'll learn who he is."

"He just gave me an orgasm and then told me we're done—that's who he is," I mutter.

Henry almost chokes on his vodka.

Feliks chuckles. "You're just as stubborn as he is. This is going to be fun."

"You probably shouldn't be in here telling me all of this. If he finds out you've been hanging with the enemy, there'll be hell to pay. Just ask me."

Feliks grins. "I will always have my pakhan's back. But I can also be a good friend to you too. I don't like taking sides." He sighs. "It's so boring."

"Do you need me to stay?" Henry asks.

"I couldn't expect that of you. You've already done so much."

"Don't be crazy. I'll ask for some time off and hang out with you for a bit. I mean, if the pakhan agrees."

"He probably won't agree, just to piss me off," I mumble.

"I'll have a word with him," Feliks offers. He drains his glass and stands.

Henry looks concerned and says to Feliks, "You don't need to put yourself in the firing line."

"Relax, I'm probably the only person in the world who isn't afraid of him when he gets like this." He gives Henry a small but suggestive smile. "Besides, I think it might be nice having you around for a bit."

When he leaves, Henry runs a comforting hand up and down my back.

"Bring me up to speed."

"He wants to look after me and the baby, but that's as far as our interactions will go. Which is fine by me. There are plenty of other things I'd rather be doing than interacting with him."

"Are you sure? Because the chemistry I witnessed between the two of you earlier was off the charts."

He's not wrong. But then, chemistry has never been an issue between us. It's been there from the very start of us and even now, as we come to the end of us, that chemistry doesn't show any sign of dying.

But that chemistry confuses things. *Clearly.*

I think about the intense orgasm I just had up against the wall and feel myself flush with both anger and longing.

"That won't be a problem," I say, and I mean it. Because if Lev is going to treat me the way he just did, then I don't want him in the same room as me, let alone close enough to touch me. "He will stay out of my way, and I will stay out of his."

32

LEV

"I think you need to give Brooke a break," Feliks says, waltzing into my study.

Five minutes ago, I was sitting behind my desk, enjoying the numbness brought on by the four vodkas I had just downed. That was until my irritating cousin decided to walk into my study and tell me what a dick I'm being.

Which makes me more petulant than I'm already being.

Because I'm not blind, I know I'm being a dick. Doing that to Brooke. Treating her that way. But I can't seem to control it. I see her, and everything hurts, and I am programmed to avoid pain.

And I don't need this *mudak* reminding me what a fucking nightmare I've created for myself.

"She seems genuine," Feliks adds annoyingly.

"Does she?"

"You don't believe her?"

"I believe she's a good actress."

She'd have to be to fool me into thinking she felt something for me. Oh, I know she felt everything for me in bed. My little bunny wasn't shy in letting me know what felt good and how I made her feel, usually crying it out when I was making her come. But I thought she felt something for me outside of my bed too.

But that was just one of a series of mistakes I made the moment I laid eyes on Brooke Masters.

"You still think she's lying?" Feliks asks.

"Of course she is. She wouldn't be the first person to tell me what I want to hear when I've caught them out in a lie."

"Well, I believe her."

"You're the one who brought me the pictures of her talking with the FBI agent. You're the one who told me Bastik was denied parole. You're the one who convinced me her betrayal was real. And now you're telling me you believe her?"

Christ, my head hurts. And not from the vodka. It's from the exhaustion of denying my feelings toward her. Yeah, I've drunk enough vodka to admit it.

"Sure, I presented the evidence. Doesn't mean she's guilty."

"Oh, she's guilty, alright," I murmur, bringing my fifth vodka to my lips and knocking it back.

This isn't like me. I never drink to the point of inebriation because I like to remain in control at all times. But fuck it. Tonight, I need it to take the edge off.

"What about the informant Agent Michaels said he had in the bratva? Has your contact mentioned any more of it?" I ask Feliks.

"No, that avenue of information has dried up. But I've reached out to Olivia to see if she can help me."

"And?"

"She hasn't gotten back to me."

"Try again," I snap, pouring another vodka from the bottle sitting on my desk.

I tell myself I will drink this one how vodka is meant to be drunk. Sipped and savored. But it's a lie. I down it as soon as I finish pouring.

"You might want to go easy on them," Feliks says.

"Why, so I can linger in the joy of my reality?"

"No, because getting drunk isn't going to make this any better."

"That is true." I pour another. "But fuck it feels better than being sober."

33

BROOKE

It takes me hours to get to sleep, and even then, my dreams are broken and obsessive and full of images of Lev telling me he no longer wants me.

I wake up in a sweat. Summer is coming, and the nights are getting hotter.

I roll over and feel the empty space next to me. I slide my hand across the cool sheets and curl into the pillow. When I slept in his bed, even when he was gone, his comforting scent still lingered in the sheets. But these sheets smell like soap and no one.

The loneliness is unbearable because I know what I am missing. Two months ago, I didn't know what his warmth next to me at night felt like. I didn't know how protected and safe and cared for I felt. When I woke up and felt the weight of him lying in the bed next to me.

But now that it's no longer an option, it feels like I have lost something special.

I sit up and hug my pillow. It's dark, but moonlight fills the room and stripes the floor.

Despite the heat of the evening, my sweat cools on my skin and I shiver. *I don't want to be alone.*

Maybe it's the emotion of the lingering pain, or perhaps it's the cold longing coiled around my body that makes me swing my legs over the side of the bed and walk toward the door.

I'm wearing nothing but a sheer nightgown as I open the door and creep down the landing to Lev's bedroom. He might turn me down. He might yell at me and turn me away. But I can't stand one more moment missing him. This ache. This longing. I would rather him give me a reason to hate him again than sip from the cup of this midnight poison one second longer.

His bedroom door is closed, but it is unlocked when I try the handle. I open the door quietly and creep inside. The room is dark. Quiet.

Empty.

He isn't here.

I walk to his bed where, only days ago, he held me as I slept. Where he made love to me with deep emotion. Giving me one orgasm after another until my body was weak and exhausted from coming.

In my memories, this room is warm and comforting, a place of love.

Now, as I stand in a ribbon of moonlight and stare at the empty bed, the room grows colder and colder.

I miss him.

I want him.

I pull back the covers and slide in between the sheets and curl myself into his pillow. His scent settles over me, and my longing for him crashes hard through my body.

I hold his pillow tighter as the tears begin to fall, and quietly cry myself to sleep.

34

LEV

I spend the rest of my night in my office, lying to myself that I'm being productive when, really, all I'm doing is trying to avoid going to my room and lying awake in my bed, torturing myself with images of her.

Tension tightens my shoulders, and my lower back aches. I'm so fucking tired. The effects of the vodka wore off hours ago when I decided I was better off working than drinking.

We are no closer to finding Vlad, and the frustration is only fueling my permanent bad mood.

We should have him by now. But the snake has slid off into the abyss.

Hide all you like, motherfucker, but I am going to smoke you out.

I won't rest until he's on his knees in front of me, pleading for his life and begging for forgiveness for what he's done.

I run a palm across the nape of my neck. But it's not Vlad who's on my mind tonight. If I'm honest, it hasn't been Vlad on my mind for the last few days. Every second, every minute seems to solely exist so I can think of her and how it felt to hold her when I fell asleep. How I would wake up in the morning and she would be there, her warmth fooling me into believing that I could have something so beautiful and precious—that it could remain untouched by the darkness of my world.

I fucking ache for her.

And nothing I do seems to kill that ache inside me.

Because Brooke is no good for me. She is a weakness, and I can't afford to indulge in weaknesses when I'm heading into battle.

Out in the hallway, the old grandfather clock chimes two o'clock in the morning. My head tells me to stay up and keep working, but my body protests and tells me to get my ass to bed.

And let's not acknowledge what my heart urges me to do.

I'm not going to her.

I won't let her in.

In an attempt to drown out the annoying voice in my head—the one that tells me to go to her—I leave my office to go to bed. I've made up my mind. No turning back. No thoughts about her lying only a few doorways down from my bedroom. But even as I take that first step on the staircase, my lust crashes through me, wanting her.

Needing her.

And it takes all of my strength to turn left instead of right at the top of the stairs.

My bedroom is dark except for a sliver of moonlight peeking in through the curtains.

That's when I see her.

She's lying on my bed, cuddling my pillow. Her breath soft. *My sweet bratva lullaby.*

No.

She's not that anymore.

The closer I get to the bed, the tighter the knot in my chest squeezes.

She's kicked off the blankets. She's wearing nothing but a slip that is so sheer I can see her skin underneath. The hem has slid up to the top of her thighs. I can see the swell of her firm breasts. Her tight nipples. That soft mound between her thighs.

Lust rages through me. But it's not the strongest emotion crashing into me right now. There's another more potent emotion, vying for my attention. *Craving.* It's so powerful it's making me dizzy. *You could join her*, it tells me. *You could end this agony by simply climbing in behind her and pulling her into your arms.*

I sweep my gaze over her again.

No, there's no going back, no matter how much my heart wants it. I would rather have this agony of longing than feel that stab of betrayal and heartbreak when she decides she doesn't want me again.

I pull the blanket up over her long legs to her waist.

Then quietly leave the room.

∼

I don't sleep. Instead, I take my car and drive around the city, hoping the sights and sounds of my favorite city in the inky early hours of the morning will calm the venom roaring in my veins. I don't know how long I drive for. But sometime after sunrise I find myself outside the apartment of Agent Michaels.

I watch him leave right on seven o'clock, and follow him as he goes about his morning routine. He wolfs down a coffee and bagel from Bernie's Coffee Stop. Then smokes a cigarette outside the diner before picking up a paper from a newsstand near the subway.

There is a lot I could do to this asshole.

I could wait in the shadows, and when the moment is right, grab him and slide a blade across his throat, and watch him bleed out on the ground at my feet.

Or I could kill him slowly with bullets to various parts of the body that would give him a slow and painful death. Parts of the body like the knees and the stomach.

But killing him would be too good for him. He doesn't deserve the peace it would bring.

No, before I'm done with him, he will know the sting of losing something he loves and all the pain that follows.

Just as he has done to me.

35

BROOKE

He's not there when I wake up the next morning. Which is actually good because, in the stark light of a new day, I can see that my coming to his room last night was a big mistake. It blurred the clear line he drew in the sand yesterday when he used my own desires against me to pay me back for running away.

Feeling stupid, I quickly sneak out of his room and hurry along the hallway to my own room. But like the universe is conspiring against me, as I approach the staircase, I walk straight into Lev, who is coming up the stairs. I take a step back, and we eye each other like enemies.

Which I guess we are.

He's made that very clear.

It's then I notice he's still wearing the same clothes he was wearing yesterday. His shirt is open far enough I can see the Zarkov tattoo across his chest, and his hair is messed up.

Maybe it's the hormones getting the better of me, but I suddenly wonder if he's been with another woman. After all, I was the one who got off yesterday afternoon, and he wasn't. And I had felt his arousal. Felt the hard outline. Saw the carnal flame in his eyes. Heard it in his voice. His desire was a wildfire burning hot and fierce.

But he didn't want me.

Immediately, my jealousy gets the better of me. Did he take care of it himself, or did someone else do it for him?

He never came to bed. Where was he all night?

I'm not a jealous person by nature. Or suspicious, come to think of it.

Maybe if I had been, I might've seen what a philandering jerk Wilson was—

No, I'm not going to apologize for being trusting and naïve. I'm done with beating myself up because of other people's actions.

I'm also not going to let this jerk in front of me make me feel something as heavy and consuming as jealousy.

"Miss Masters," he says with a sharp tone.

"Mr. Zarkov."

He towers over me, and I'm suddenly caught in his heat. His scent. That dark gaze.

"Were you looking for me?" he asks, his voice too controlled.

His gaze sweeps over my breasts and my hard nipples poking through the flimsy fabric, and all I can think of is how his lips used to wrap around them and suckle and lick until I begged him to fuck me. I quickly wrap my arms around my chest to cover them, my cheeks growing pink under his heated gaze. Does he think of that, too, when he looks at me that way?

Does he remember how good it felt to slide his tongue over the perky nub and suck?

My lips part, and my breath quickens. The air between us is tight with unsaid words and unquenched need. The way he is looking at me. My body recognizes being this close to him, and she couldn't give a shit about hating him right now.

Damn hormones.

Instinctively, I take a step back, and his eyes flare, and his jaw clenches.

"Yes, I want to see Igor," I blurt out.

He nods curtly.

"I have assigned a detail of three men to you. If you choose to go to the hospital, then you are to speak to Pierce and have him organize the detail for the day." His words are clipped and cold. *Unfeeling.* "You do not leave this property without clearing it with him first."

I look into his eyes to see if I can find any trace of the man I'd slept next to last week before I fled. The man who pulled down his walls for me, only to rebuild them because he thinks I betrayed him.

But he is gone, and in his place is a cold robot.

If only he would talk to me without it becoming an argument.

If only he would believe me.

Trust me.

I'm ready to forgive him for not trusting me if he can forgive me for leaving.

"Lev—"

"If that is all, then I have things to do."

He brushes past me, and I turn to watch him walk away.

"This is just so easy for you, isn't it," I call out.

He pauses with his broad back to me. He lifts his head but doesn't say anything before he finally walks off.

~

After my run in with Lev at the top of the stairs, I go straight to my room to put on something a little less *nipply*, then go in search of Henry. I find him in one of the palatial bedrooms sliding his bag over his shoulder. He looks like he's ready to walk out the door.

"You're leaving?"

"I'm sorry, baby girl. I thought I'd be able to get some time off, but I don't have enough vacation time, and HR are being real dicks about it. I have to be in the office first thing in the morning."

"But you can't leave," I cry.

"I will be back as soon as I can." He walks over to me and gives me a warm hug. "Besides, I think you and Lev need some space to figure things out."

"We live in a palace. Space isn't the issue."

"You know what I mean."

"If you leave I might actually murder him," I whisper dramatically.

He winks. "Or kiss and make up. *A lot*."

"Doubtful."

"He's hurt."

"I didn't betray him."

"That's not why he's hurt." He gives me a look like I'm missing the point. "You ran, and I don't think he realized just how deep that was going to cut him."

"You got all of that from the small amount of time you spent with him?"

"Sweet thing, I got that in the first five minutes with him. He's in love with you."

My eyes go round. "In love—"

"Head over heels. Smitten kitten. Batshit crazy for you."

I fold my arms across my chest. "Crazy is right."

"He needs time."

"He needs a lobotomy."

Henry gives me a pitiful look as if I'm a lost cause but he doesn't have the heart to tell me. "Give it some time. Right now he's like a wounded bull. But in a few days he'll be more approachable."

It's not a bad plan. Avoid Lev. *I like it.*

"What am I going to do without you?"

He presses a kiss to my forehead. "You're going to figure things out. I promise. Besides, I'm just a phone call away."

Watching him leave with Feliks fifteen minutes later, I suddenly feel all alone. I miss my friends. *I miss Lev.*

Urgh, I hate this.

To avoid running into his lordship, I get out of the house as soon as possible and visit Igor at the hospital. With my best friend gone, I feel even less inclined to spend time at the mansion with the grumpy pakhan.

I leave the house irritated by the way Lev is treating me, but when I arrive at the hospital, my mood immediately changes from being agitated by Lev's mere existence to one of cold heartache.

Because Igor is still so sick and seeing him lying on the bed is a stark reminder of how everything can change on a dime.

One minute you're walking toward your car. The next, your body is broken and you're fighting for life in a hospital bed.

Thankfully, he's out of danger. He will live. He's still on a ventilator and bandaged from head to toe. But the doctors are confident his lungs are healing enough for him to be able to breathe on his own soon.

When Enya visits the cafeteria for coffee and to stretch her legs, I sit beside him and take his hand in mine. And for a while, we just sit there, and the only sound is the machines keeping him alive.

Finally, I huff out a breath and let the words tumble out.

"Sorry I left. I got scared. But I shouldn't have left. I should've stayed and tried to figure things out. It's just that I'm not used to this world, and I got scared because… I'm pregnant, okay, and I had to think about the baby. Did you hear that, Igor? I'm having a baby. Lev's baby. And I need you to wake up. Because I'm going to need your help keeping Lev from being over-the-top protective as my belly grows bigger." I try to keep my tone upbeat. "You know how crazy possessive he can get. I mean, look at how he reacted when I stole his car…"

A sudden wave of grief and fatigue hits me, and I choke back a sob.

"Please wake up," I whisper.

I press my forehead to the top of his hand and let the exhaustion of the last week crash through me.

Igor's finger moves and brushes my cheek.

I lift my head. "Igor?"

He's still unconscious, but his finger definitely moved.

"Can you hear me?" Again, his little finger moves, and I start to laugh, but tears prick at my eyes.

He's going to make it.

I call the doctor, and a team of medical staff pile into the room, and one of them ushers me out so they can examine him. I stand at the viewing window, waiting anxiously for an update.

I wrap my arms around my waist. Surely, this is good news. Surely, this is a sign that he's healing.

I feel Lev before I see him. It's like a sixth sense. *Or a dark cloud.* I turn to look down the corridor and see him exiting the elevator, looking elegant and composed in a fresh new suit. He's shaven, too, and my heart sends out a protest that the beautiful man walking toward me no longer wants me.

Our eyes meet, but his expression doesn't change. It's cold and unfeeling.

I know things are bad between us. But none of that seems to matter right now. Not with Igor improving.

"He's waking up," I say to him when he joins me at the window. "I think they're removing him from the ventilator."

Only now does his expression lose its cold edges. "Has the doctor said anything?"

"No, they ushered me out of the room, so I don't know anything. But I was talking to Igor, and he could hear me. I know he could. He moved his finger. He knew I was crying—"

Levs frowns. "You were crying?"

He looks at me, concern in his eyes.

But I have to look away. Because if I don't, I'll cry. Thanks to these damn hormones and the fact that the man standing next to me has built a floor-to-ceiling wall around his heart and seems determined to keep me out.

"According to my pregnancy hormones, I seem to have a lot to cry about."

He shifts his gaze from me to look into Igor's room through the window, and I see his jaw harden.

The silence and tension between us are so thick you'd need a chainsaw to cut through them.

"Are you going to give me the silent treatment forever?" I ask. "We're having a baby—"

"And I've told you that I will provide for you and the baby." He stares straight ahead as he talks. "You will want for nothing."

"But I want you."

My words rattle him. Oh, he does his best not to show it, but I see that flicker of humanity and pain on his robotic face.

But when he slowly turns his face to me, they are gone. "That is not an option."

His words aren't spoken cruelly. Just with cold, harsh fact.

"Fine. When you're over your tantrum, you know where to find me."

When I try to walk away, he takes me by the arm. "What you said earlier is not true. This isn't easy for me. It's not fucking easy at all."

Hope blooms in my chest. "Then talk to me."

He lets me go. "I've said all I intend to say about the topic."

"Then you're a fool."

And without another word, I walk away.

36

BROOKE

They remove Igor from life support but keep him heavily medicated. He's not out of the woods, they explain. He needs to heal. So I spend the next few days with Enya at his bedside. I'm keen to put some space between Lev and I, but I also want to support my new friend as she waits for her love to heal and wake up.

On the day Enya has to go to an appointment, I decide to stay with Igor and read to him. Because I've heard reading to unconscious people helps them heal quicker. Or wake up. I'm not sure on the details. But I figure if he hears me talking to him it might bring him some kind of comfort.

Besides, the silence is killing me. Without distraction, my thoughts go to Lev, and I'm tired of him taking up the real estate in my head.

So I go in search of a book in the waiting room, but there is little to choose from. Just a pile of old magazines, and I'm not sure how interested Igor would be in *Ten Ways to Know He's Cheating*, or *How to Make the Perfect Meringue*.

A nurse walks past and asks what I am looking for, so I explain my idea to her even though it sounds crazy saying it out loud.

Her face lights up. "I have a book in my bag that you could read to him. I just finished it on my lunch break. It's a mafia romance though. Do you think he'd mind?"

I grin. *How appropriate*. "I couldn't think of anything more perfect."

Back in Igor's room with the book, I get comfy and start reading.

The first chapter flies by, then the second, and the third, and then I'm so engrossed I'm a third of the way through the book before I even realize.

I don't hear Lev until he speaks. "Are you seriously reading him a romance novel?"

At the sound of the grumpy pakhan's voice, I almost jump out of my skin. I turn to see him standing in the doorway. Fresh suit. Hair perfect. Looking like a boss.

"Yes, I told him if he didn't get better then I was going to read it to him. It was only a threat. I was only going to subject him to the first chapter, but damn, this book has sucked me in. It's a mafia romance so you'd probably like it."

He cocks an eyebrow at me as he looks at the title. "The Devil's Den."

"It's about a ruthless mafia don. You should read it. Who knows, you might pick up some tips."

"Nice cover."

"It's spicy too."

"I'm sure Igor is thrilled," he drawls.

He turns his attention to Igor and his jaw tightens. I see the flash of pain in his expression, and I know it hurts him to see his friend so unwell.

I don't know what to say to him, and the silence is deafening, so after a while I pick up the book and start reading to Igor again.

I expect Lev to leave. But he doesn't. He sits down, and it's confusing because I don't know how I fit into this scenario. What I should do, if I should leave. But I get the feeling he doesn't want me to leave, that right now this is what he needs, to be with his friend. And if I am really honest, I don't want to leave. It's nice to be in the same room as him without all the tension and frosty silence. It's like Igor's room has become neutral territory where we can co-exist without arguing.

So I keep reading, and Lev listens, and before too long he's giving a running commentary.

"Yes, that is exactly what I would do."

"What does she expect, he's mafia, of course he's going to do that."

"Yes, I would shoot him for touching her too."

And it's so surreal because he's giving me a glimpse of the man he was before I ran away. The man he's kept hidden from me since I returned. *The man I fell in love with.*

When I get to a part where the hero is keeping the heroine locked in a bedroom and her sassy reaction to it, he cocks and eyebrow and mutters, "Oh, how I can relate, my friend."

But it's all too much when I get to a spicy scene. Lev stands and moves toward the door.

"But we're just getting to the good bits," I say.

He shakes his head. "No, the good bits were in the beginning before he fucked up and fell in love with her."

∼

Two days later, summer turns up with vengeance. It's like God turned up the heat overnight which is a stark contrast to the frostiness that still exists between Lev and I. Despite the mild thaw that happened after we spoke at the hospital, for the last couple of days we've done a superb job of avoiding one another.

Which is fine by me.

If he's determined to think I'm some kind of rat, then I'm determined to stay out of his way until he's ready to see sense and apologize for being a dick.

But today the sun is bright, the sky is blue, and I refuse to let Lev's bad attitude ruin my mood. I decide to head down to the humongous pool to enjoy the sunshine. It's the perfect opportunity to try out the new bikini I bought online after Lev told me he didn't want me asking him permission every time I want to make a purchase.

Buy what you need, Miss Masters. I don't want to hear about it.

I slip on the bikini. I've always been curvy, but standing in front of the mirror, I can't help but admire the way my body is getting curvier with the pregnancy. Full breasts. Soft thighs. A growing belly.

I twist and turn in front of the mirror, and my new bikini shimmers with a hundred different shades of aqua.

I glide my palm over my round tummy. It's not big yet. But it is rounder. And there's something magical about knowing there is a tiny life growing in there.

Today marks the beginning of my second trimester, according to the checkup I had yesterday. Thankfully my morning sickness is gone, along with the persistent fatigue. In fact, I feel amazing.

I can't help but grin at my reflection. I'm so in love with the baby inside. I can't wait to be his or her mama. I can't wait to hold him or her in my arms, and sing to them, soothe them, and let them know how loved they are.

I have no idea how Lev fits into all of this. I know he'll make sure we want for nothing. There's no doubt about that. Because he is more than generous with his money and his things. It's just when it comes to showing me any emotion that he's completely bankrupt.

Which is fine by me, because I'm still pissed at him for thinking that I betrayed him to the FBI. I was prepared to let it go for the sake of the baby. But he's right when he calls himself a tenacious fuck. Every day, he retreats further away from me, and it's wearing thin.

And to be honest… I miss him.

I miss what we had before I left. The closeness. The tenderness. The late nights staying up talking and learning about one another.

Not to mention the molten sex.

My body throbs hungrily at the memory of those nights spent in his bed. Now that my morning sickness is gone and I'm further along, my sex drive is off the charts. Which is unfortunate now that I don't have anyone to satisfy the craving.

Throwing on a sheer linen shirt over my bikini, I grab my sunglasses and water bottle and leave the room.

The swimming pool at the Zarkov Estate looks like something you'd see in a resort. Palm trees line the outside of the pool and white sandstone is stark against the crystal blue water.

I sit on one of the many sun loungers and slip off my shirt.

I know in here I am free from the prying eyes of Lev's men. They do not patrol the pool. But they certainly control every inch outside of the six-foot walls that surround it.

I remember Lev telling me once that this pool is his sanctuary during the hotter months. This is where he likes to swim laps first thing in the morning, and he likes to do it undisturbed by prying eyes.

I sigh. Here, I am safe from everything and everyone.

I lie down and relax on the sun lounger and enjoy the warm sunlight on my skin. After a few moments, I decide I don't want the tan lines of my bikini top and undo the bow that holds it in place and let it slip to the ground beside me. I glance around, making absolutely sure that there is no one around, and slide off my bikini bottoms, too, and they fall to the ground beside my bikini top.

Fully naked, I stretch out along the sun lounger.

I love my pregnant body. I love how it's softened. But the pregnancy hormones, well, they are something else. One minute I'm fine. The next, I'm either cleaning crazily, crying because of a sad commercial on the TV, or I'm so fucking horny I have to get myself off just so I can walk straight.

And right now, while I'm stretched out naked under the sun, my body feels needy for a release. *No, it's needy for cock.*

That's another thing I purchased in my online shopping haul. Thick. Eight inches. And fully hard. My new friend has helped me out immensely when it comes to satisfying the ache.

But right now, I need to be touched. I need to be kissed and caressed, and I want *him* to do it. There's no shame in it. Because a woman has needs. And this pregnant woman has a lot of them. But he is not an option. No matter how hard my nipples have gotten or how swollen and wet I am down there just thinking about him.

It's either my hand or my battery-powered boyfriend, and that's in the nightstand in my bedroom.

I glance around the pool area.

There's no one around.

Slowly, I let my hand drift down between my legs.

37

LEV

Oh, hell, no.

From behind my desk I watch the image on the screen in front of me. It's from the camera in the pool area. Dressed in my swimming shorts, I was about to head down to the pool to do some laps when the image from the security camera caught my attention.

In the pool area, Brooke is stretched out on one of the sun loungers, her beautiful body tanned and smooth, her belly swollen with my baby—

And she's fucking naked.

My entire body stiffens with possessiveness, and I have to remind myself that my men are not required to patrol that side of the wall.

No one can see her but me.

I stand at the monitor and watch as she drags her fingertips up and down her torso and over the soft swell of her breasts before finally heading south and disappearing between her thighs.

I look down at the front of my shorts where my cock is straining to get out, then look back to the camera monitor.

Christ, she looks good.

Tanned skin. Soft thighs. Heavy breasts.

She's wearing sunglasses, so I can't see if her eyes are open or closed, but her glossy lips are parted, and her chest is starting to rise and fall as her arousal grows.

This is fucking torture.

I need to either join her poolside and take her on the sun lounger, or I need to sit behind my desk and take care of this myself in the privacy of my office.

Poolside is not an option.

Because it wouldn't be enough.

One taste and I'd be doomed. It's why I'm in this goddamn nightmare to begin with.

I sit down behind my desk and turn the monitor so I can watch her.

Opening the top drawer, I remove the soft scarf Brooke left in my office weeks ago and wrap it around my hand and wrist as I inhale her scent off of it. The other hand slides beneath my shorts and grips the base of my cock.

On the screen, Brooke's hand works between her thighs, and I groan, knowing how sweet and wet her pussy would be. I work my hand up and down the length of my cock, rolling my palm over the head to spread the precum across my skin for lubrication.

Watching her is torture. Because watching her makes me want her, and right now, that want is going to get me into a lot of trouble if I'm not careful.

I tip my head back and focus on the ceiling instead. I stroke slowly, building the tension in my balls. I take my time. Find pleasure in the buildup. Bring myself to the brink and then pull back.

When I'm ready to come, I close my eyes and press the scarf to my face, and Brooke's scent is like a drug, making me high with images of her riding my cock with that sweet pussy of hers, those full breasts slick with sweat, her luscious lips parted as she moans my name, over and over, and—

I let out a groan at the exact same time there is a hesitant knock on my door.

My eyes flick open and dart to the monitor.

Brooke has left the pool area, and it doesn't take a genius to figure out who's standing on the other side of my door.

I'm only a few strokes away from coming, so taking my hand off my cock is as enticing as eating a bowl of razor blades. But I grit my teeth and let go, exhaling heavily through the discomfort with flared nostrils.

I readjust my shorts and shove the scarf back in the drawer. "Enter."

The door opens, and Brooke appears. She's wearing a white linen shirt over an aqua bikini, and her cheeks are flushed. *Because she just made herself come beside the pool.*

My cock throbs, reminding me we have unfinished business.

She looks hesitant. "Do you have a minute?"

I try to look aloof and in control. But really, inside, I'm desperate to bend her over my desk so I can ease the ache in my balls and satisfy my unquenchable thirst for her.

"What can I do for you, Brooke?" My tone is all business, but it's all lies. I'm barely in control, I'm so fucking turned on. Before, she was just an image on the screen, but now she's warm-blooded and real, standing in my office wearing a bikini that shows off her glorious curves and cheeks flushed from the orgasm she gave herself, and dammit, this is a fucking nightmare.

She approaches the desk. "I wanted to ask if I could start buying things for the baby nursery."

"You have a credit card. You've been shown the room where the nursery will be. You have full control over it."

"I know, it's just, I thought you might like to be included or have some say—" Her eyes widen when she sees the feed from the pool area on the monitor. "Is that the pool area?"

No point in lying. "Yes."

Her eyes dart to me. "You've been watching me?"

"Yes."

If it's even possible, the pink in her cheeks deepens and her eyes grow wider. "You saw me?"

"Yes."

She licks her lips and I can't keep my eyes off them. *Damn, I want a taste.*

"You watched what I did?"

I can't keep the smirk off my lips because she's so fucking gorgeous when she squirms. "Yes."

She puts her hand on her hips. "So much for privacy."

"Perhaps now is the time to tell you that there isn't an inch of this estate that I can't see," I tell her. "Not one inch I don't control."

"That information would've been helpful ten minutes ago," she mumbles.

I rise to my feet and move around the desk toward her. Her gaze brushes over the front of my boardshorts. She can see I am hard but quickly averts her eyes. Which makes me smile.

"No point in getting shy on me now," I say, closing the space between us.

I should tell her to leave, but the mere scent of her is awakening the part of me I'd planned to never let see the light of day again. The part that aches for one more kiss. One more touch. One more time to bury myself deep inside her. That part of me wants out. It's ready to do anything to break free. And I'm so hard, I can't hold it back.

Perhaps I was too quick to push her completely out of my life. After all, there's no law to say I can't keep her at arm's length *and* enjoy her body in my bed.

She lifts her chin. "What's a girl to do when she's not getting it from anywhere else? Other than the battery-powered boyfriend I recently bought online."

She bought a vibrator?

That'll be going.

Because I've decided from now on, if she needs satisfaction, she'll get it from me.

"You want satisfaction, I'm happy to give it to you."

"I can barely get you to look at me, let alone fuck me," she snaps, reminding me that I've been an ass to her lately by ignoring her.

I could make it up to her. Pay her back in pleasure. I know it's not enough, but it's all I've got to offer right now.

I move closer. "Let me extend the open invitation."

"Oh, I'm supposed to just climb onto your cock now because you order me to, is that it?"

"No, I want you to climb onto my cock because I know you want to." I lock eyes with her. "Tell me I'm wrong. Tell me those bikini bottoms aren't soaked. That your body isn't craving the kind of orgasms only I can give you."

Her eyes sharpen. "You arrogant—"

"Tell me it wasn't me you were thinking of when you rubbed your pussy."

"It wasn't—"

"Liar." It's written all over her face. *And damn if that doesn't do something to me right now.* "Tell me it wasn't my name on your lips when you slid your fingers into your sweet pussy and fingerfucked yourself into an orgasm."

She hesitates, and if looks could kill then I'm a dead man.

But I ignore it. Because you can't kill a man whose heart is no longer beating.

Instead, I kiss her hard. And when she tries to fight me, I hold her face in my hands and take the kiss from her. She struggles at first, to prove a point, but then kisses me and doesn't hold back.

"This doesn't mean you're not an asshole," she says between kisses.

"Oh, I know." I lift her up in my arms and walk us back to my chair. "You should take it out on me."

She straddles me. "No, you would enjoy it too much."

She lifts her linen shirt over her head, then leans forward and kisses me.

Damn it feels good to have her in my arms. To feel her lips on my lips.

"Did you like watching me?" she rasps, her sweet body grinding against me.

"Yes." I groan because I'm not even inside her and I'm already fighting the urge to come.

"Tell me what you liked." She runs her hand over the rigid outline of my cock. "Tell me what made you hard."

She starts to massage my already straining cock, and I have to fight back the orgasm I'm on the brink of falling into.

"You," I groan. "Always fucking you."

I reach up and loosen the bow holding her bikini top on, and it falls to the floor, exposing her beautiful, creamy breasts.

I take one nipple in my mouth and suckle, then do the same to the other, and the soft cries coming from Brooke are almost my undoing.

She undoes the bows at her hips so her bikini bottoms slip away, and I push down the front of my shorts and release my cock. She licks her lips at the sight of the bulbous head and the precum pooling in the eye before she maneuvers herself above it and slowly sinks down.

We both groan at the same time.

Fuck.

Buried deep inside her is exactly where I belong.

I might not know how any of this fits together in the puzzle, but I know I don't want to give this up.

She rides me and I can't keep my lips off her. I drag my tongue along the curve of her slender throat, relishing the taste of her skin.

Her hips gather speed, and her moans grow louder, until she falls apart on top of me. "Lev...oh God..."

It's all I can take. Being inside her. Hearing her moans. Tasting her skin. Being consumed by the warm, sweet scent of her after days of denying myself. I let go, and my orgasm rips out of me. I hold her tightly against me, and my roar is primal and hot and angry and grateful all at the same time.

Brooke collapses against me, her body warm and soft, and I can't help but hold her as I drift back into reality.

But the moment her breathing evens out, she climbs off me and puts her bikini back on. She's angry. And I'm not sure if she's angry at me or herself.

"What are you doing?" I ask.

"Leaving."

"You're fucking and running. That's cold, Miss Masters."

"Cold? That's rich coming from you, Mr. Frosty." She slips the linen shirt over her bikini. "You've had me living in an arctic purgatory for the last week, but then the first sign of any warmth from you, I jump right into your lap like a horny idiot. This is why I have a vibrator. Less complications."

"So you're angry at me for wanting to fuck you, and angry at yourself for letting me?"

Her eyes shoot laser beams at me. "Yes, I'm angry at you. And yes, I'm angry at me. And since I can only get away from one of the two people pissing me off right now, I'm leaving."

I don't exactly know what I am expecting from her right now. Her leaving is probably a good idea. But going by the knot in my chest, that's not what I want.

Because you want her, you fucking fool.

Just admit it and put this sorry bullshit behind you.

But instead, I let my hurt do my bidding for me. "Well, by all means, feel free to come back and get your fill from me whenever you want."

Her eyes and mouth widen. But she slams her mouth shut and slays me with a glare. "Fuck you. This was a mistake, one I won't be repeating."

"Until you're horny again."

"You —"

"I know, I'm an asshole. But I'm an asshole with a big cock and I know how to use it to make you come over and over again. And I'm only too happy to do that, anytime, day or night."

Her jaw tightens. I'm hurting her, and I can't stop, because damn, nothing hurts like the woman you love leaving you, and the monster it awoke is an ugly, miserable beast, and is angry as fuck.

Who fucking knew I was capable of feeling this way. Not fucking me.

Her eyes narrow. "I won't be your fuck buddy, if that's what you're suggesting."

She turns to leave, and I feel like a jerk.

I don't want her to leave. "This is all I'm capable of right now."

She fixes me a look that could melt glaciers. "Well, forgive me if I feel I'm worth a little bit more than that."

And she storms out, slamming the door behind her.

38

LEV

The following morning, I take large strides along the hospital corridor on my way to Igor's room. Half an hour ago, I got the phone call to say that he was awake and sitting up, and I left for the hospital the moment I ended the call.

When I reach his hospital room, the relief I feel when I see him propped up against the pillows and eating the ice cream Enya is feeding him is more immense than I can describe. It's like a part of me can goddamn breathe again.

They've removed a lot of his bandages, and the color has returned to his face. Apart from a few scrapes and bruises, he's looking good.

I hover in the doorway.

He sees me, and when our eyes meet, I wonder how the hell I am ever going to make any of this up to him.

Enya sees me and puts down the ice cream. "Look, pakhan, he's awake, and look how strong he is."

Igor gestures me over to him, and when I reach the bed, he holds his hand up for a goddamn fist bump.

So I goddamn fist bump him. "You look good, my friend."

He manages a small smile. "The doctors say I will get out of here within a week."

"Then I'll make certain you have everything you need when you do."

I know his rehabilitation is going to take some time. But I will put everything in place to ensure he receives the best treatment.

He turns to Enya, who is smiling brightly. Her eyes have finally lost the sheen of worry, and I can see the love and affection in them when he takes her hand. "When I get out of here, we're moving in together," he says.

Well, I'll be damned. My giant friend has finally found his queen. It makes me happy, and I'll make sure they want for nothing. "That sounds like a very good idea."

The door opens, and Brooke walks in carrying a tray of coffees. I haven't seen her since she stormed out of my office yesterday afternoon. She stalls when she sees me and then quickly moves toward Igor and Enya where she makes a point of handing out the coffees.

Last night, during those dark hours when everything seems so much worse, I was tempted to visit her in her room. To apologize for being an ass. To beg her to tell me she didn't rat me out to the feds. To tell me she didn't leave because she doesn't love me. Because I'm fucking in love with her and damn if it's the hardest thing to stop doing, especially in the middle of the night when I want her next to me in my bed.

But I didn't, because some things are best left unsaid.

"You should get some rest," I say to Igor. "I'll come by tomorrow."

I give Enya a wink but avoid making eye contact with Brooke as I leave the room.

But if I thought I was getting out of there without speaking to her, then I was mistaken. As I head toward the elevators, she calls out my name. I turn around and watch her walk down the corridor toward me.

"Is there something you need, Brooke?"

"About yesterday afternoon—"

"You were right to walk out."

She looks surprised that I am being so agreeable. "I was?"

"It complicated things."

She nods. "It did."

An awkward silence falls between us, full of all the things we want to say but don't because we are too damn stubborn.

Or proud.

"Is everything okay with the baby?" I ask. "I got your message about the doctor's appointment next week. I'll drive you."

"You don't have to."

I step closer and put my hands on her belly. "I'm going to be with you every step of the way through this pregnancy."

When I look into her big brown eyes I feel an ache in my chest. I mean it. I will be there through all of it.

I don't remove my hands. Because being this close to her and my baby is the only way to tame the pain I feel when I think of a future without her in it.

"Do you need anything?" I ask.

"I'm fine. And no, I don't need anything, other than…"

"Other than what?"

"For you to stop being angry at me for something I didn't do."

I want that too. Because after days of aching for her, I've decided I want to believe her. I want to *trust* her. Because I'm in love with her. *Deeply*. But I was programed from a young age not to trust so easily, and this need for caution is ingrained deep in my soul. Trust has to be earned, and when all the evidence points to betrayal…well, here we are.

But that doesn't stop me from wanting to put this behind us. I just have to figure out how.

"We'll talk, just not right now. I've got something I have to do."

Surprising us both, I pull her closer and plant a kiss on her head, savoring the scent and closeness of her, before taking a step back and walking away.

When I reach the hospital parking lot, I call Feliks.

"Call Olivia in the FBI and set up a meeting right away. I don't care what you have to do to make it happen. Sell her a goddamn kidney if you have to, but make it fucking happen."

39

LEV

"So, when was the last time you saw her?" I ask Feliks.

We're standing in a tunnel in Central Park, waiting for his contact at the FBI to join us.

"A while," he says sheepishly.

"So there's a chance she might stand us up?"

"She'll be here."

As if on cue, an attractive redhead in a serious trench coat and killer heels walks up to us. Feliks steps forward to give her a kiss, and she turns her head so it brushes her cheek.

"When I said call me, I didn't mean eighteen months later," she says smartly.

"You look stunning, Olivia," he says.

She flashes him a look. "Your flattery will get you nowhere."

Ten seconds in her company, and I can already tell she's a no-nonsense woman. She's all business, and I doubt she's easily intimidated.

I offer her a hand. "Lev Zarkov."

She has a solid handshake. "Olivia Vega. Nice to put a face to the name. Feliks always spoke so fondly of you." She shifts her gaze to Feliks. "I found the information you wanted. She gave a statement."

I grit my teeth. What Brooke said in that statement will be able to be used against me. "I need to see it."

"Statements are sealed," Olivia says.

"Not to someone of your caliber," Feliks says.

"Again, flattery won't get you anywhere. Eighteen months ago, maybe, but not now."

"What will it take to unseal it?" I ask.

She thinks for a moment, then replies, "Dinner at Edgewater." She locks eyes with Feliks. "For me and my husband. It's our one-year anniversary in two weeks."

Feliks' brow lifts. "You're married?"

"Well, it got tiresome waiting for you to call."

"Consider it done," I say. "I will make the arrangements."

Olivia gives me a pointed look. "There's a six-month wait to get a booking. You'll never pull it off."

I give her a smile. She really doesn't know who she is dealing with. "You will have the details within the hour."

She tilts her head. "Feliks always said you made magic happen. I guess we'll find out."

"I guess you will."

Her immaculate red lips spread into a slow smile. "Fine."

She removes a folded piece of paper from inside the breast pocket of her trench coat and hands it to me. "Agent Michaels never submitted the statement. But it was found on his phone right after he was fired."

Feliks looks surprised. "Fired?"

"Because Agent Michaels couldn't come up with any credible evidence of your alleged crimes, he falsified his reports so he could keep the case active. Then his supervisor discovered Michaels had used his credentials to get a family member's drug possession charges quashed. Not once, but a total of four times. The FBI doesn't like that behavior, and unfortunately for Michaels, this family member was involved in a much bigger ongoing case, which means Michaels tampered with evidence. He'll probably do time. Looks like Lady Luck is on your side, Mr. Zarkov."

The last part has nothing to do with luck. I had one of my investigators look into Agent Michaels' past for something I could use against him. It took a while to find something on the over-zealous agent, and for a while I thought I might actually have to kill the mudak for fucking with my life. But once I got my hands on the information, I knew I wouldn't have to waste a bullet.

I made sure the damning evidence made it to the director's office and waited for the fall out.

Fallout achieved.

Michaels was fired.

You fuck with me and my girl and I will take you down.

I look down at the piece of paper in my hand. "This is what she told Agent Michaels?"

"Word for word," Olivia replies.

My jaw tightens as I read Brooke's words.

Lev was nothing but a gentleman during our time together, and I have no knowledge of any criminal behavior that you claim he orchestrates.

She didn't betray me.

I re-read the statement before handing it to Feliks.

"We heard Agent Michaels claimed he had an informant in the bratva. Do you know who it is?" I ask.

Olivia shakes her head. "There isn't one. It was another one of his lies. Michaels fabricated the claim when the director questioned the solidity of the case he was building."

Fuck.

"You have some loyal people in your camp, Mr. Zarkov. You're a lucky man. Loyalty can be hard to come by nowadays."

I give her a curt nod, because right now, I'm not sure I even fucking deserve Brooke's loyalty.

Feliks releases a slow whistle. "Well, damn. She was telling the truth."

"Thank you," I say to Olivia. "You went out on a limb, and I won't forget it."

"No, you won't. Because you'll be sending me those dinner details."

I resist a smile. "You have my word."

I like this woman. She's a bit of a ballbreaker. She would be an asset in the Zarkov camp.

"Well, gentlemen, I need to get back to the office," she says.

"Thank you," I say to her.

She nods and walks away.

"I owe you one," Feliks calls out after her, but she doesn't look back as she leaves the seclusion of the tunnel and disappears into the sunlight.

"God, why didn't I call her?" Feliks asks.

"Because you're an asshole," I reply.

He turns and presses Brooke's statement into my chest. "Yeah, seems there's a lot of that going around."

Feliks is right. I am a fucking asshole.

I pushed Brooke away because of this.

What the fuck have I done?

40

LEV

I'm angry at myself.

No, I'm fucking *furious* at myself.

Brooke told me she didn't tell the FBI anything, and I didn't believe her. If I'm really honest, I didn't want to believe her, because believing her would require me to trust her, and I have a hard time doing that.

Trust people and you give them the chance to hurt you. I learned that lesson early, and it's done a good job of keeping me alive.

Not that Brooke is a threat to my life. Just that wild, beating mass of muscle and blood vessels pounding in the middle of my chest. It was easier to build a wall around it when I thought she had betrayed me than it was to let her in, and for the first time in my life, I took the easy option.

Dammit, I've made a fucking mess of this.

"You know this is going to require some serious groveling," says Feliks as he drives.

He's right. I'm going to have to think of something pretty special to make it up to her. And something tells me that my little bunny isn't going to make it easy on me. And she shouldn't. I've been a fucking ass.

Deciding to send her a text, I pull out my phone, but it starts ringing. It's an unknown number. My shoulders go tense. A burner phone. In my world, they mean trouble.

I answer it, and I don't recognize the voice on the other end because it's been distorted. "You want to find Vlad, then come to the corner of Eagle and Albion in Brooklyn."

Two seconds after the caller hangs up, my phone beeps with a message. He has sent me a picture of Vlad. He's sitting in a chair. And he is very, very dead.

Feliks spins the car around and takes off in the direction of the address the mysterious caller gave us.

"It could be a trap," he warns.

"It probably is, but I'll organize some men to meet us there."

It takes us twelve minutes to get there. The address is an old canning factory on the waterfront that's been abandoned for years. Some developer bought it but hasn't done anything with it yet.

We should wait for my men to get there before we go in, but they are still five minutes away, and I'm an impatient fuck, so we enter the building and make our way through the empty factory.

We find Vlad in the old administration office. He's sitting in the chair with a bullet in his forehead.

"Well fuck," Feliks says, kicking a broken waste basket on the ground next to the door.

I'm seething. "Who the fuck got to him before I did?"

I hear someone behind us and swing around.

Vadim steps out from the shadows. "Hello, Nephew. I think we need to talk."

41

BROOKE

I leave the hospital to run some errands and spend the next couple of hours shopping for baby items. But I'm so distracted by what just happened with Lev at the hospital, I can't concentrate.

Yesterday afternoon I was angry at the both of us for what happened in his office so much I couldn't sleep for it and I was prepared to keep being angry.

But today there was something different between us. The ice has thawed. And when he placed his hands on my stomach they had lingered, and I had felt something between us. The same feelings we had before I ran. I could see them in his eyes. Feel them in his touch.

I need to talk them over with someone. So when I receive a text message from Enya asking me to join her for an early dinner at one of the bratva's restaurants, I jump at the chance.

The restaurant is a popular venue on the waterfront, but when I arrive, it looks closed. The sign on the door says it doesn't open until five o'clock, but Enya's message specifically said to meet her here at four.

Perhaps they're opening early for us?

As I approach the doors, they open, and a beautiful woman welcomes me in with a big, glossy smile. She's gorgeous. The kind of *beautiful* you can't help but stare at. Wearing a silk suit in the deepest navy and a pair of Jimmy Choo stilettos, she looks a little overdressed to be a waitress, but leads me through the restaurant to a table outside on the deck.

While I'm being seated, one of the two bodyguards Lev insists I take wherever I go, leaves to do a perimeter check, while the other sits far enough away to allow me some privacy.

"Can I get you some water while you wait?" the beautiful lady asks in a thick Russian accent.

I don't know why, but a cold, uneasy feeling crawls up my spine.

I let out a heavy breath and tell myself to get a grip. *I'm safe.* Still, I can't help but glance at the bodyguard sitting mere yards away.

I give the server a smile. "No, thank you, I'm fine for now."

She walks away, and I open the menu, but it's all in Russian. Enya will need to translate it for me. Which makes me think that perhaps I need to learn Russian. No doubt Lev will want his son or daughter to speak it, and I should probably learn too.

I'm typing myself a note on my phone to look into online Russian language courses when a shadow falls across the table.

I look up and see Boris smiling back at me.

Instantly, my nerves are calmed. Behind him, I see Maksim talking to the lady in the silk suit. She touches his arm intimately, and I get the feeling that they know each other well.

"Brooke, how delightful to see you," Boris says. "May I join you?"

I smile up at him. "Please have a seat."

I'm sure Enya won't mind Boris and Maksim joining us. After being at the hospital all day, Boris' jovial demeanor might be exactly what the doctor ordered for all of us.

Boris sits and rests his big, meaty hands on the table in front of him. But Maksim doesn't sit. Instead, he stands beside his father, and unlike his father, he's not smiling.

The uneasy feeling I felt earlier returns.

Something isn't right

"It's lovely to see you," I say to Boris, trying to push back my sudden unease.

He smiles but there is no warmth. "Do you like my restaurant?"

I glance over to my bodyguard but he isn't there, and a strange sensation begins to tingle in my stomach.

Get out.

I smile but it's weak. "Oh, yes, it's beautiful." I pick up my phone, look at the dark screen, and then put it down again. "But unfortunately, it looks like I've been stood up. Enya just messaged me to say that she can't make it. Looks like we'll have to reschedule dinner."

I stand and pick up my handbag and tell myself not to make it obvious that I'm freaking out. That there was no message from Enya. That I'm terrified because something in my gut tells me to run.

But I feel Boris' eyes on me, and my hands start to shake.

"Sit down, Brooke," he says calmly.

"I really must get going," I insist.

"I said sit down," Boris says again, this time with an edge in his voice.

My mind racing, I slowly sit. "Is everything alright?"

It suddenly occurs to me that something might have happened to Lev, and Boris is here to tell me that my life is about to change again. Because whoever was after him finally got him, and now he's dead.

God, I feel sick.

"Has something happened to Lev?" I ask, unable to hide my panic.

Maksim breaks his stony facade with a chuckle, but it fades when his father shoots him a look.

Boris turns his attention back to me. "For now, he is unharmed."

For now?

"What does that mean? I don't understand."

Boris gives me a smile, but there is something off about it. "Before I tell you what I came here to tell you, I want you to know that this is nothing personal. I like you, Brooke, I really do. But unfortunately for you, you were in the wrong place at the wrong time."

The way he's looking at me—the way they are *both* looking at me—pours fire on my fear and ramps it up to the next level.

Again, I scan the room for my bodyguard. But he is nowhere.

"Your bodyguard is dead," Boris says, as calmly as he would say, *pass the salt*. "He put up a struggle, but he was no match for Maksim."

Fear tightens like a tightly coiled spring in my chest, and I find it hard to swallow for the ginormous lump of fear lodged in it. "What are you talking about?"

"I'm sorry, Brooke. But you're a loose end that needs tying off."

I shake my head. My heart is pounding so hard I almost can't hear him over the roaring of my pulse in my ears. "I don't understand."

"If only you hadn't gotten pregnant with the heir to the Zarkov fortune and head of the table. I would've simply executed Lev and let you leave. But I can't let that baby in your womb take a single breath. It is a threat to me and my sons."

Sons?

Oh my God, is Feliks involved with this too?

"What are you gonna do?" I ask, my voice trembling.

He nods to Maksim, who clicks his fingers, and the beautiful lady in the silk suit reappears, but this time she is hustling a bound and gagged Enya into the room.

I forget about my own fear for a moment. "What do you think you are doing?" I demand. "Get your hands off her."

Silk Suit shoves Enya toward me.

"Sit down," she commands.

With a whimper, Enya sits in the chair beside me. Her wrists are bound in front of her, and her hands are shaking. Our eyes meet. She's been crying, but other than that, she looks unharmed.

"It's going to be okay," I try to reassure her, but my voice trembles because I'm not sure that is true.

I glance around the empty restaurant, looking for signs of help, but the place is empty.

"No one is coming for you," Maksim says coldly. "Your fiancé is otherwise detained."

My gaze darts to Boris. "What have you done to him?"

He waves it off as if it's nothing. "Just a mild distraction to ensure that he is nowhere near here."

I lift my chin. "So what happens now?"

"Now I move the final pieces into play."

Fear is a bullet zipping through every part of my body.

He's going to kill us.

"Let Enya go. She's not involved with any of this. Why is she even here?"

"She was a means to an end, I'm afraid, my dear. We needed to lure you out from the safety of the mansion. We were only going to take her phone so we could send you the message. But she caught one of my soldiers lifting it from her bag while she was in with Igor. Now, she will join you in death." He sighs. "Another case of being in the wrong place at the wrong time. Three minutes later and she would be looking for her phone now, not living her last few minutes here with you and me."

Enya whimpers around her gag, her eyes wide and frightened.

"You don't need to do this," I say in a low, calm voice I don't even recognize. But it comes from a place of strength, that part of me that will do anything to save the life of my baby. "Let us live, and we will go away, and you will never see either of us again."

"I'm afraid it's too late, Brooke. The die has already been cast."

He doesn't seem sorry at all. He's just toying with us and getting off on it, the sick fuck.

"Please," I whisper desperately.

"Now, don't go and do that," Boris snaps. "Don't go begging. You're stronger than that. Given the chance to live, you would have been a great wife for the pakhan. I admire your strength, so don't let it fail you now. I will make it quick. There's no need for the two of you to feel any pain."

Beside me, Enya whimpers again, but it's not fear—she's calling him something nasty in Russian that I don't understand. Her eyes are hard and sharp.

"Now, now, no need for name-calling," Boris says, turning his attention to her. "This is how it has to be."

He removes his gun from the breast pocket of his suit and sits it on the table in front of him. Fear blasts through me, and I have to bite back a cry of panic. I let out a rough breath in an attempt to control my quivering chin.

God, he's going to kill us here.

The sudden shrill of the fire alarm makes me jump. Boris turns to Maksim. "Go check it out."

Maksim obeys, leaving us alone with Boris and Silk Suit.

The odds are against us, but we have to try to stop this from happening. I look at Enya and gesture with my eyes to Silk Suit. Enya's eyes tell me she understands. I know there's very little chance what I'm about to do is going to work out. But I won't go down without a fight.

I give Enya a nod, and the moment she swings her legs around to topple Silk Suit off her feet, I flip the table.

It takes Boris by surprise, and his gun falls to the floor.

We both go for it at the same time, but I'm smaller and faster, and I reach it first. I hold it up, but I don't have any idea what I'm doing with it.

Silk Suit gets Enya in a chokehold, so I point it at her. "Let her go."

"Or what, you're going to shoot me?"

Enya elbows her in the solar plexus to break free. With a growl, Silk Suit goes for the gun concealed in an ankle holster, so I shoot her.

Honestly, I don't mean to shoot her. It's almost a reflex action. It gets her in the leg, and I watch with wide eyes as blood begins to spill down her silky pants. It's enough to stop Boris from lunging at me. He steps back, arms high. But I know it's only a matter of time before Maksim comes running back in, so I grab Enya, and we both flee down the stairs leading to the parking lot. I hear yelling behind us. Heavy boots clomp along the deck, and I aim the gun and just start firing randomly to buy us some time. In a matter of minutes, this place will be swarming with Boris' men.

When we reach the parking lot, we stop briefly so I can untie Enya's hands. She rips the gag out of her mouth. "Those motherfuckers, we should have shot them all."

"There will be plenty of time for that later." When Lev hears about this, he will rain fire and brimstone down on his uncle and cousin.

That's when I think about Feliks. Is he involved with this too? Did he conspire with his father and brother to murder Lev?

I look around in a panic for an escape route. The parking lot is empty, and I don't know what to do. I hear the fire alarm stop and voices shouting inside the restaurant. They're coming, and we've got no way of getting out of here.

It's then I hear the screech of tires and the roar of a car engine, and I turn and see a car barrel toward us. It stops with a skid in front of us, and inside is Vadim. I take a step back.

No.

"Get in," he demands.

Both Enya and I make a run for it. And I hear Vadim growl as he chases after us in the car. He comes roaring past us and blocks our exit out of the parking lot. I aim the gun at him, but it's empty.

He pulls his weapon on Enya and me, and I'm pretty sure his has bullets in it. "Get in the fucking car."

I want to cry. We've come so far only to be stopped just before we reach freedom.

Enya and I do as he tells us to, and we climb in the car. Vadim barely waits for us to close the doors before he roars out of the parking lot and onto the road.

I look behind us as Boris and his men descend onto the parking lot.

Did Vadim just save us?

I turn to look at the old Russian.

"You're not taking us back to Boris?"

His face is unreadable as he looks at me.

His phone rings, and I watch as he brings it to his ear. "I found them."

42

LEV

I meet Vadim under the bridge on the waterfront. When he pulls up, Brooke opens the back door of the car and rushes toward me, flinging herself in my arms and holding me tight.

It's only now I realize I've been holding my breath.

"Oh God, I was so scared," she cries into my neck.

I tighten my arms around her. *Me too.*

The rage flooding my veins comes second only to the relief I feel that she is out of danger and in my arms.

I inhale the subtle scent of her and close my eyes. I would burn down the world for this woman.

She gasps when she sees the car parked a few yards away from us. Inside, two armed men keep an eye on us. It's my security detail.

"Who are they?" She cries.

Midnight Poison

I hold her tighter and press a kiss into her hair. "They're here to protect us. You're safe now."

I don't want to let her go, but she takes a step back. She has questions.

She swipes at the tears streaming down her face. "I don't understand what's going on. I thought Boris and Maksim were the good guys."

"No, I was wrong to trust them." The words are hard to say because I know this mistake almost cost me everything. "It was Boris who organized the hit on me. He and Maksim have been conspiring to get rid of me."

My relationships with my uncles made me blind to the truth. Boris was always the fun-loving uncle and seemingly disinterested in the prestige of being pakhan. Whereas Vadim was always aloof and resentful, or so I thought, and this prejudice made me oblivious to the fact he was working all this time to uncover the truth and expose the lies.

"Boris wasn't the man everyone thought he was," Vadim says, walking toward us. Enya walks beside him, looking shaken.

"But how did you know he was the one behind all of this?" Brooke asks.

"I always suspected Boris was up to something," he says as he reaches us. "He is my brother, and I've always known what he was. As kids, he was the sneaky one. Conniving. The one who hid his crimes behind his charm and an easy-going smile. But in reality, he was cold and ruthless, with no regard for life. He liked to hurt things. Animals and humans. He was always in trouble. But he got smarter as he got older, and as an adult, he hid those dark urges behind a fake jovial persona. Everyone loved him, but I knew the real Boris. I knew what kind of evil ran in his blood. That kind of darkness doesn't just go away."

"You've been watching him?" Brooke asks.

Vadim nods. "One day, I saw him meet with Vlad Bhyzova, and I knew Boris was getting ready to do something. It was a gut feeling. Like I said, I know my brother. So I used Vlad's arrogance and vanity to get closer to him so I could find out what Boris had planned. I appealed to Vlad's need for recognition as someone important, and he lapped it up, the stupid *mudak*." Vadim's eyes sharpen. "It was tiresome listening to him go on about himself and how important he thought he was. But I knew if I waited long enough that he'd slip up, and I didn't have to wait long. One night, after too many vodkas, he told me things were about to change. He didn't say what, but he did say that the cracks in the bratva were about to widen. I knew it involved Boris, and it confirmed my suspicions that he was going to make a move to overthrow Lev."

"Why didn't you say anything to Lev?" Brooke asks.

"Because I didn't know what was being played out. All I had were my suspicions, and I figured if I kept playing along, Vlad would slip up again, and I would find out something concrete. But in order for that to happen, I couldn't risk Vlad or Boris or Maksim figuring out that I do support Lev as pakhan. I had to keep them thinking that I was at odds with it."

Brooke nods and nestles deeper into my shoulder, gnawing on the inside of her mouth as she processes everything he is telling her.

"Vlad is dead," I tell her.

"How?"

Vadim replies, "I received a text message with an address. When I arrived, I found him dead."

"Boris sent me and Feliks there too," I explain.

"But why send all three of you?" Brooke asks.

Vadim glances around, scanning the waterfront and the shadows under the bridge for any signs of approaching danger. "I think he knew I was onto him."

"And he sent Feliks and me there as a distraction to keep us occupied while he—" I stop. She doesn't need a reminder of what she just went through.

Vadim steps forward. "But it worked against him. When I told Lev and Feliks my suspicions, we realized Boris had orchestrated it so there would be some kind of altercation between Lev and me. Something that would keep his focus on bratva business and not you."

I add, "When we found Vlad, I called you. But when I couldn't get hold of you or the bodyguard assigned to you, I knew something had happened. And I knew that something was Boris."

Brooke lifts her gaze to me. "Feliks isn't involved?"

I shake my head. "No."

She doesn't look convinced. And who can blame her. "Are you sure?"

"He was as in the dark as Vadim and I were."

Her brow furrows as she tries to understand everything we're telling her. She looks to Vadim. "How did you know where we were?"

But it's me who answers. "After Vadim told us about Boris, the three of us split up to look for you. He knew Boris did business at the restaurant he owns on the waterfront."

"More than a couple of bodies have been floated out to sea from that restaurant," Vadim adds.

Brooke swallows thickly. "He was going to kill us and put us into the ocean?"

She looks pale.

I want to get her to a doctor.

I weave my fingers through hers. "But it didn't happen."

She nods, but I can see her racing pulse in her neck.

"You set off the fire alarm at the waterfront?" she asks Vadim.

"Yes."

"It saved our lives."

"We were outnumbered. I had to cause a distraction and hope you could use it to your advantage."

"Thank you, Uncle," I say.

He saved the love of my life today.

Brooke turns to me. "Where's Feliks?"

"He's due to meet us here, but I'll message him and have him meet us at the house," I explain as I pull out my phone. The last time I spoke with Feliks was twenty minutes ago when I called to tell him Vadim had secured Brooke and Enya. "I'm also going to call the doctor and have him meet us at the house, because I want him to take a look at you."

"I'm fine," she insists. "Just shaken."

I give her a soft smile. "Humor a paranoid father-to-be. I'd rather be certain you and the baby are okay."

She nods, and I pull her into my arms again, looking up at the sky and thanking whatever entity is up there for looking out for her today. *I owe you one.*

I turn my attention toward Vadim.

"Make sure Enya gets home safe. We will meet you there."

The sun is getting lower. It will be dark soon, and I want to get Brooke home where it's safe. Boris and Maksim are still out there, and we're vulnerable out here.

Vadim leaves with Enya, and Brooke climbs into the Escalade beside me.

I still have to tell her about what I learned from Agent Olivia Vega. And I know I'll have a lot of groveling to do to make things up to her. And I will. I'll spend the rest of my life working to make her trust me again. *To forgive me.* But right now, I just want this. The relief of knowing that she's safe.

As I drive out from under the bridge, I take her hand and secure it in mine. "I'm not letting this go again."

"I don't want you to. Not ever."

She smiles at me, and I know I am going to love this woman until my last breath and beyond.

It's the last thing I think before the crash comes out of nowhere.

And without warning, my world goes black.

43

LEV

I wake up in the back of the car with Brooke beside me. She looks dazed but unhurt. She's sitting in between me and Maksim. In the front, one of Maksim's soldiers is driving while Boris is beside him in the passenger seat.

I groan, and Boris looks at me over his shoulder.

"Ah, the great pakhan is finally awake. I was worried for a moment. Thought we nudged you too hard off the road and you'd sustained a head injury. Fortunately for us all, it is only a bump." He claps his hands together. "Now, we can finally put all this ugly nonsense to an end."

Blood drips into my eye from a wound to my brow, and I feel nauseous and dizzy, but I force myself to focus. "Let Brooke go. It's me you want, not her."

Next to Brooke, Maksim snickers. "She carries the heir. She's not going anywhere."

"Not to mention she's a witness, and isn't that one of the mantras you live by, Nephew? *Don't leave any witnesses.*" Boris shakes his head. "Except you haven't been living by your own rules lately, have you, Lev?"

My head throbs with pain, and it takes me a moment to realize he's talking about Wilson.

"You know about Wilson," I mutter, looking out the window. There's no point asking about my security detail. If I'm in here, then they're dead.

"I've had eyes on you for months as I formulated my plan to take control of the bratva, and you know, I was surprised when you let him go. But then I met Brooke, and it all made sense. Our mighty pakhan had gone and gotten himself pussy whipped." He roars with laughter, and even Maksim chuckles. "She's made you weak, Lev. She's made you go against your better judgment. And it's your fault she is here."

"You won't get away with this," I tell my uncle. "The inner circle won't stand for it."

"Oh, but they will. When they hear how you attacked us because you were out of your mind, they will understand that it was in self-defense. After all, they witnessed you lose control in the meeting when you pulled a gun on Vadim in front of them."

"Vadim will set them straight. He knows what you've been up to all along."

Boris' mirth leaves him. "He will be another dead body you will be blamed for before the day is done." He points out the windshield. "Pull in here, and let's get this done."

We turn off the road and take the gravel driveway down to an old warehouse. Once we stop, Maksim and Boris hustle us inside while the driver remains in the vehicle.

This tells me he's on watch for anyone coming. Which means there's a good chance there aren't too many soldiers around.

Inside, it's dark, and it takes a moment for my eyes to adjust. The warehouse is dimly lit and empty, and I can't see any more soldiers.

Boris takes us to a small room, an old office, similar to the one where we found Vlad earlier today. It's empty of furniture. Water drips down the brickwork, and the air is musty. When we walk in, we step onto plastic.

It's easy to dispose of bodies when all you have to do is wrap them up in the plastic they died on.

I don't feel fear.

I feel rage.

Because Brooke shouldn't be here. She wasn't a part of this until I took her for my own selfish reasons.

She deserves more than this.

And our baby. He deserves to take his first breath. To feel sunlight on his sweet face. To grow into a man who is much better and a fucking lot smarter than his father.

Keep him talking. Stall him for time.

Feliks and Vadim will come looking for us.

"How does Vlad fit into all of this?" I ask.

"Vlad was an idiot. We recruited him, but then he went rogue on us. Kidnapped Brooke because he couldn't contain his resentment toward you. He thought it would earn him our respect, when all it earned him was a bullet. He strayed from the plan. That's when everything fell apart. It made him a liability."

"So you killed him," I mutter.

"And sent you and Vadim looking for him so I could meet with your bride." He grins. "She's a feisty one, I'll grant her that. I wasn't expecting her to get the better of me and my men. It was an annoyance, but at least we're all here now."

"Except Feliks isn't here. He was with Vadim and me. He knows what's going on and won't stand for it. What are you going to do, kill your own son too?"

Boris nods to Maksim, and my cousin leaves the room, returning a moment later with Feliks, who is gagged. He shoves him into the middle of the room and removes the rag from around his mouth.

Feliks spits at his brother. "You motherfucking—" Maksim shuts him up by shoving the rag into his mouth before moving away to stand by his father. Feliks spits the dirty cloth out and glares at his brother. "*Mudak*."

"What is this, a family reunion?" I ask, stalling for time and trying to process the scene so I can figure a way out of here.

But Boris knows what I am doing. He chuckles, his eyes sparkling with menace.

"Family? You want to know what I think about family? They get in the way."

The way he says it makes something click in my head, and my nostrils flare.

He's talking about my father.

"*You* had my father killed."

"Of course I did. And Vadim was supposed to be with him." His face twists into an ugly scowl. "Then I would've had a clear path to become pakhan."

"But you didn't know my father had declared me as his successor and that he would deny the bratva the hefty inheritance he had bestowed them in his will if they didn't vote me in."

His eyes flare with anger. "It was a thorny detail I was not anticipating. Not only did I have Vadim to deal with, but I had you as well. So I decided to start fucking with the both of you. Pit one against the other. While I remained the fun-loving uncle stuck between the two. I needed a war because it's easy to hide the body count amongst all the bloodshed. A death here. A death there. My claim for the role of pakhan wouldn't be as obvious."

"Except Vadim had you all figured out."

"Perhaps, but I knew you hated him enough to never believe him."

I shake my head. After all this time, the man who murdered my father was the man I called Uncle. A man I trusted. "My father loved you."

He scoffs. "Like I said, Nephew. Family just gets in the way."

He nods to his son, and Maksim lifts his gun and shoots Feliks.

Brooke screams as Feliks falls to the floor, and I feel a bolt of panic rip down my spine.

"He's your son," I yell at Boris.

"My *second* son. Not my heir. He sealed his fate the moment he became your right-hand man."

I glance at Feliks on the floor. He's not moving, and his eyes are closed. I move Brooke behind me. They're going to have to get through me to get to her.

"So this is it? You're going to kill us all so you can be pakhan?"

Boris grins. "Yes, and then, when I've served my time, Maksim will step in."

"Actually, Father, there's been a change of plans," Maksim says.

Boris jerks around to look at his son. "What are you talking about?"

Maksim raises his gun again and shoots his father in the head, and Boris drops heavily to the floor, blood spilling out of the bullet wound between his eyes.

Behind me, Brooke gasps and takes a step back.

Maksim stands still, looking at his father's body before he finally lifts his cold stare to me. "He was right. Family does get in the way."

Fuck. Me.

All this time my charming cousin was an unhinged psycho and I never even knew.

"What are you doing, Maksim?"

"I'm doing what I have been bred to do. Taking my seat at the head of the table. It's what he always wanted. It's what I was raised to do. But I figured, why wait for the old fuck to die when I could just do it myself? Of course, the plan was to do it after he'd done all the heavy lifting. Disposing of bodies is time-consuming and tedious. But today, I realized he was just weighing me down, and I was better off without him." He focuses on Brooke. "I mean, the fat old fuck had you in the palm of his hand, and he let you get the better of him." He shakes his head. "I decided right there and then I had to get rid of the old fool sooner rather than later."

I see Boris' gun in his suit jacket.

"You'll be dead before you even reach it," he warns.

I've got nothing left. So I use the last thing I have in my arsenal. *My body.* I charge at him with the fury of a wounded bull. He tries to aim his gun, but I reach him before he can get a shot off and tackle him to the floor.

We roll around in the mud, and I get a few good slams of my fist into his evil, smug face. But somehow, the sonofabitch is able to knee me in my balls, and I curl up into the fetal position.

He retrieves his gun off the floor and rises slowly to his feet. "You never could admit defeat. Even when we were kids you always had to win. But today is the day you finally lose, *pakhan*." He walks over to me and aims his gun. "Your time is up, *mudak*—"

A gunshot explodes and reverberates around the room, and he drops to the floor like a house of cards.

I look over to Feliks, who still has his gun aimed at his brother.

"Motherfucker," he moans before slumping against the floor and falling unconscious.

44

BROOKE

As Lev makes a phone call, I kneel beside Feliks. Blood soaks the front of his shirt, and when I rip it open I see a small hole in his chest, high up near his collarbone. Blood bubbles to the surface and keeps spilling over his skin.

His eyes flutter, and he wakes up with a groan.

"He needs an ambulance," I say to Lev, who is speaking very quickly to someone on the other end of the phone.

Feliks grabs my arm. "No ambulance."

"But you need medical treatment, and you need it fast," I say to him, applying pressure to the gunshot wound to try and reduce the bleeding.

"Then drive me to the hospital. No ambulance." He looks over my shoulder. "He'll never be able to make this go away if you call an ambulance."

I follow his gaze to where his brother and father lie dead on the floor, only a few yards away.

"I'm so sorry, Feliks," I say, understanding how heartbreaking this must be for him.

He grimaces. "I'll live." He drops his head back and moans. "Well, I fucking hope I do."

Another gunshot makes me jump. Alarmed, I swivel around to look for Lev but he's gone.

"No need to panic." Feliks assures me, biting back his pain as he holds up his gun. "I've got your back."

I take the gun from him because the more he waves it around, the more his wound bleeds.

"I can't shoot it if I'm not holding it," he complains.

"But I can. Don't worry, I'm practically an expert after today."

My nerves calm when Lev returns.

"What was the gunshot?" I ask.

"My uncle's driver. Don't worry, he's not going to be a problem anymore." He lifts Feliks to his feet. "Come on. There's a hospital not far from here."

Feliks lets out a grunt of pain. "Fuck, I think I'm going to pass out."

"You're not going to pass out," Lev says calmly, slowly walking him out of the building.

"I feel woozy."

Lev helps him into the car. "Better feeling woozy than feeling nothing because you're dead."

Ten minutes later, we make it to the hospital. Fifteen minutes after that, Feliks is rushed into surgery.

I pace the waiting room while Lev talks to the medical staff. "That's my best friend in there," I hear him saying in that powerful voice of his. "I don't care how much it costs or whatever you have to do—he survives this, you got it?"

When he joins me in the waiting room, he looks exhausted.

"Is he going to make it?" I ask.

Lev pulls me into his arms, and I can see the worry in his eyes. It's the same worry I feel knotted in my stomach. "He has to."

I lay my cheek against his chest and find comfort in the rhythmic hammering of his heart. And it's how I stay for the duration of Feliks' surgery, listening to the heavy pounding of Lev's strong heartbeat, praying Feliks makes it. Because I don't know how Lev will be if he loses him too. By now, he'll be feeling the pain of his uncle and cousin's betrayal. He lost two people close to him today. Two people he loved but who didn't love him back. The sense of betrayal will run deep in him.

There is so much left unsaid between us, but now is not the time for talking. Now is the time to pray Feliks makes it through his surgery.

Finally, the doctor appears. "He's going to be fine. The bullet missed his heart and lungs, so he'll make a full recovery."

I feel the tension ease out of the both of us.

"Can we see him?" Lev asks.

"Not until tomorrow. He's heavily medicated and needs rest."

Lev nods, and the doctor leaves us.

"Come on, let me get you home," he says, taking my hand.

We're both quiet during the car ride home. There's a lot for the both of us to unpack. Lev has the weight of his uncle and cousin's betrayal resting on his shoulders, while I'm still trying to process everything from having my life threatened at dinner, to being kidnapped and threatened at gunpoint in a derelict warehouse somewhere in the city at sundown.

And if that wasn't enough, somewhere amongst all of it, is the hurt I feel because Lev didn't believe me when I needed him too. Although, in the grand scheme of things, it feels easier to let it go now.

You would think after everything I've been through since the fateful day I met Lev on the plane that I would be getting used to unpacking all the shit that's been happening to me. But I haven't, and worst of all, I know being with him means there will always be things to unpack if I continue to share my life with him.

But I also know that whatever lies ahead will be worth it. Because I've had a taste of life without him, and there is nothing that could be done to me in the future that would make me want to drink that midnight poison again.

By the time we make it back to the Zarkov estate, it's dark.

In Lev's bedroom, I lie on the bed and watch him remove his shirt and jacket.

"I read your statement," he says, kicking off his shoes.

I sit up.

"Statements are sealed—what am I saying, of course, that would never stop you." I cross my arms. "So I guess about now you're realizing what a giant asshole you are."

"Something like that."

I lift an eyebrow. "I'm waiting for the apology."

"Oh, it's coming, *zayka*. Every day for the rest of our lives if need be."

"Good. And don't think I'm letting you off that easily," I say.

"I don't expect you will."

"You hurt me."

His face softens as he walks over to the bed and gently brushes the backs of his fingers across my cheek. "I know, and I'm sorry."

There is more to say. But after the events of today I don't have the energy.

I take his hand. "Don't think this conversation is finished."

"I know I have some making up to do," he says.

"Yes, and it starts right now." I pull him down to me. "Take off your pants, Mr. Zarkov. Because showing me just how sorry you are starts right now."

45

BROOKE

It's the happiest I've ever seen Lev in... well, forever.

Gone are the tense shoulders and the grumpy scowl, and in their place is a man who isn't afraid to show the world he actually has teeth. His smile is devastatingly handsome, and I like knowing that I help put it on his face.

This morning, I woke up in his arms, and it felt like a new beginning. Like all the darkness is finally behind us, and we can look forward to a future together. *The three of us.*

Now it's evening, and after a day spent enjoying each other in all the sexiest, yummiest of ways, we're walking down the hospital corridor toward Igor's room.

But it seems our friend doesn't share our lighthearted mood. When we walk in, Igor is arguing with the nurse. He wants to go home, and he wants to go home *now*.

"Leave us," Lev says in that commanding voice of his, and the nurse does as he says.

He sits on the edge of Igor's bed. "It's not like you to give the nurses hell."

"I want to go home. I am well enough."

"That may be so, but you're still on IV antibiotics and strong medication. The doctors say you're better here than at home. They're concerned about infection."

"I will go mad if I have to stay here another second looking at these same walls and the same ceiling, day after day, night after night."

"It's only a few more days."

"Which is a few more days too long. I'd rather eat my gun."

Enya, who is walking in carrying a juice, gasps in the doorway. She hurries to put down the juice and goes to him. "What is wrong, my lion?"

"He's throwing a tantrum," Lev drawls.

I notice how Igor's mood seems to calm in Enya's presence. She climbs on the bed and wraps her arms around him, and he is instantly soothed.

"Our pakhan is right. It's only a few more days, and you can come home." She pushes her gentle fingers through his hair in a nurturing way that tells me he is going to be well taken care of when he returns home. "Until then, you have to listen to the doctors. I need you to be well, my love."

"I know the days are slow in here." Lev stands. "But as it happens, I've got something that might cheer you up."

"I doubt it," Igor mutters.

Lev chuckles. "And you call me grumpy."

"Not to your face." Igor folds his arms. "What is the surprise?"

"Well, that's the thing, I need you to come outside and take a look for yourself." He walks over to the wheelchair parked in the corner of the room.

"You're being very mysterious," Igor grumbles.

"Because I am a mysterious guy." Lev winks at him. "Now, how the hell do we get you into this?"

Because he is so big, it takes the three of us to get him out of the bed and into the wheelchair.

"I haven't seen the sun in weeks," Igor says as Lev steers him out of the hospital room.

"Then get ready, my friend, because the sun is due to set soon, and it's going to be fucking beautiful," Lev says, pushing his friend down the hospital corridor toward the elevators.

I've never seen this side of Lev before. And it makes me fall even deeper for him.

Lev is right—outside, the sun is easing lower into the horizon, painting the sky in a thousand different tones of red and gold. It's stunning.

The four of us pause to look at the brilliant sunset.

Igor closes his eyes and sucks in a deep breath, and slowly lets it go.

When he opens his eyes again, Lev is dangling a set of car keys in front of him.

"What are they?"

"A set of car keys—what do you think they look like?"

He points the wheelchair in the direction of a brand new Rolls-Royce Phantom glinting in the fading sunlight.

"You bought a new car," Igor says, his eyes twinkling as he looks at the gleaming beast. "She is a beauty. Hopefully, I will be able to return to work and drive her soon."

"No need. This isn't a car for driving me around," Lev says. "This isn't even my car. This is your car."

Igor looks from the Phantom to Lev, then back to the Phantom. "I don't understand."

Lev takes his hand and places the keys in his giant palm. "She belongs to you."

"Pakhan—"

"I was getting tired of the Phantom anyway. I think I want something else. But I'll figure that out when you come back to work in about ten to twelve weeks."

"I won't need that amount of time off work."

"Yeah, you will. After your rehabilitation ends, I'm sending you and Enya on a much-earned vacation. Anywhere you want to go."

Igor looks moved. "There is no need for this generosity."

Lev's expression is serious. "Yes, there is, my friend. You almost lost your life, and that isn't lost on me. I was always going to give you the Phantom, but fate beat me to it. This isn't me buying your forgiveness. This is me saying thank you."

46

LEV

After we leave the hospital and return to the Zarkov Estate, I lead Brooke into my office and close the door behind us.

"I'll never get over the look on Igor's face when he saw the car," she says, her beautiful face beaming with a big smile. "You know, I could get used to this soft, yummy side of you."

I lift an eyebrow. "I don't think anyone has ever called me soft and yummy before."

She grins, and it's a mix of sweet and wicked, just like her. "No, because you're usually walking around like a grumpy robot, barking orders at people and kidnapping poor, unsuspecting women from their apartments in the middle of the night."

She flutters her long eyelashes at me, and I grin as I pull her into my arms, liking the feel of her curves against my body. "The latter was the best thing I've ever done."

"Oh really?"

I glide my palm over her belly, which is growing every day, and feel a surge of love for the baby growing inside. I lift my gaze back to her. "And I'd do it all over again in a heartbeat."

She smiles, and it's gentle and warm. "I like soft and yummy."

I kiss her and feel the lust unfurl in my body. Brooke softens against me, but I break off the kiss. I didn't bring her in here for that—I've got something else I want to do. Something I've been wanting to do for days.

"I've got something for you too," I say.

Her eyes sparkle. "You do? What is it?"

I remove the small box from my breast pocket and hand it to her.

When she hesitates, I gently prompt her. "Go on, open it."

She lifts the lid and gasps when she sees the black diamond ring winking up at her.

"Oh my God, it's stunning. What is this?"

"It was my grandmother's engagement ring and her mother's before that. They say the diamond is the rarest of its kind and is said to bring an abundance of good luck to whoever wears it."

Brooke lifts her big brown eyes to me. "I don't understand. Are you giving this to me?"

I drop to my knee in front of her.

"I fucked up, Brooke. I should never have doubted you. But even I can't turn back time to fix it. All I can offer you is today and the future, and I figure two out of three isn't bad. So if you'll have me, I'll give you all of me. Everything. The good. The bad. The light. The dark. And every shade in between. No holds barred, Brooke. No doubt."

"You want me to marry you?"

"*Zayka*, I want that more than the air in my fucking lungs."

Tears brim in her eyes and spill down her cheeks.

"I'm crazy fucking in love with you, Brooke Masters. So please don't keep me hanging." I lift an eyebrow. "I don't get on my knees for anyone. But I'll get on my knees every day for the rest of my life if it means you'll say yes."

Tears stream down her face. "You love me?"

"More than fucking life."

"Then get up here and kiss me."

I rise to my feet, take her in my arms, and crush my lips to hers. She doesn't hold back. She kisses me just as fiercely and hungrily as I kiss her.

"Is that a yes?" I ask.

She nods, and I take the ring from the box and slide it onto her finger.

"I'm not taking this one off," she says through her tears.

"Good. But these…" I start sliding the thin straps of her tank top down each shoulder. "These have gotta go."

She looks up at me coyly. "Why?"

"Because what I'm about to do to you… they're just gonna be in the way."

She laughs as I continue to peel her clothes from her luscious body.

And I show her exactly what I'm talking about.

47

LEV

Because we can't wait, I marry her the very next day in Igor's hospital room with only Feliks, Igor, and Enya in attendance. Still recuperating from his bullet wound, Feliks is sitting in a chair by the door nursing the open bottle of champagne we smuggled in, while Enya lies with Igor on his bed, her tiny body snuggled tightly against my giant friend.

I wear a suit, and my stunning bride looks like an angel in a sheath of champagne satin. It clings to her beautiful curves as well as the heavy swell of her stomach where my baby is growing.

God, every time I see her belly, I'm overcome with love for her and the baby she's nurturing in her womb.

She smiles across at me, and I can see the love shining in her big eyes. She's carrying a tiny posy of flowers she picked from the garden, and I don't think I've ever seen her look so beautiful.

I'm so fucking in love with her I can barely see straight. I want the priest to hurry up and get it done so I can kiss her as my wife for the very first time.

This woman is everything.

When it comes time to exchange rings, Feliks walks over and holds up his pinkie, where two rings gleam in the dull light of the hospital room. "You're full of good ideas, my friend, but marrying this angel is the best one you've ever had." He gives me a wink, and I take the first ring from him and slide it onto Brooke's finger, promising her my devotion for the rest of our lives together.

When it's her turn to take the ring from Feliks' finger, he says with a cheeky grin, "He knows he's punching above his weight marrying you, beautiful lady, and don't you ever let him forget it."

With a grin, she slides the wedding band on my finger and vows to love me until death and beyond, and I believe every word. No more doubting this woman, ever.

I'm about to kiss her when her eyes suddenly widen, and her hands go straight to her belly.

"Oh my God... Lev!"

Alarm bells take off in my mind. "What is it? Is everything okay?"

My panic turns to relief when she grabs my hand and places it on her round belly.

"The baby... I just felt her kick." Her face beams up at me just as a little thump pushes into the palm of my hand. "There, can you feel it?"

Another thump. Then another. And another.

"Oh my God, she's having a party in there." Brooke laughs.

But I'm overcome with such an intense emotion that I can't make my lips work. It's a feeling I could never describe and one I have never known before now. It's like a rush of pride. Of pure love.

I place both hands on her belly.

My baby.

I never cried at my parents' funerals. I never cried when my grandpa died, either. In fact, I've never cried when life has kicked me in the balls and presented me with things normal people actually cry about. But right now, during one of the happiest moments of my life, I finally feel those tears pricking in the back of my eyes.

I struggle through the intense feeling, and I smile through my tears.

"My son has a strong kick."

"Your son? I think you mean your daughter," Brooke says, laughing.

I step closer so there is no space between us, both my palms still on her belly as I look down on her beautiful face. I don't care what sex the baby is. Whether I have a son or a daughter, they will be more loved than anything or anyone on this planet. And it's only now in this moment, as I feel him or her moving against my palm, that I realize I could have it all taken away from me—the power, the prestige, the wealth—and none of it would matter, as long as I have these two in my life.

"*Zayka...*" I tilt my head to kiss her, moving my hands from her belly to her jaw. "I'm so crazy in love with you."

"Good because you're stuck with me."

I smile against her lips. "Tell me you love me."

"More than life."

With a rasp, I kiss her fiercely, and she melts into me as our kiss deepens. I need to get her out of this dress and into our bed now.

It's when the priest awkwardly clears his throat that we stop. "Let's wrap this up, shall we? There'll be enough time for that."

"Then you'd better be quick, Father. I'm not sure I can hold off much longer."

I look at my wife and see the love shining in her eyes, and all I can think of is how much I will always love this woman.

She has been my best decision. My biggest win. My greatest love.

She's brought out the human in me and taught me two valuable lessons in life.

That some things aren't worth fighting for.

While others are worth giving your life.

48

BROOKE

I stretch out naked on the bed and hold up my hand to look at the wedding band on my finger. I've been Brooke Zarkov for almost three hours, and all of them have been spent in bed with Lev. After bidding Feliks, Igor, and Enya goodbye at the hospital, he's been showing me exactly how appreciative he is that I am his wife, and now my body is heavy and relaxed with the afterglow of numerous orgasms.

His phone buzzes on the nightstand, and he opens a message. Putting it down, he rolls over and places a kiss in the crook of my neck.

"I have a surprise for you," he murmurs before pulling away and climbing off the bed to redress.

"You do?"

"Yes. But you're going to need to put some clothes on," he says, his eyes still filled with carnal need as they sweep over me lying naked on the bed.

Midnight Poison

Sitting up, I look at him suspiciously. "What is going on?"

He hands me my dress. The one he'd barely gotten off me without ripping because he was so desperate to fuck me as his wife. I slide it over my head and slip on my underwear.

"I'm not sure if I should be excited or afraid," I say, straightening my dress.

He pulls me to him and looks down on my face with great affection. "You're going to love it." He drags a finger down my neck and across my cheek, coming to a stop against an erect nipple, which he begins to rub. "And later, you can show me how much you love it."

I can still feel him between my legs. A delicious ache from being pounded by my husband's talented cock. Now, a new throb has taken up there, and if he keeps rubbing my nipple like he is, then the surprise will have to wait.

God, this is going to be a great wedding night.

He grins. "Are you ready?"

When I nod, he takes my hand, and we leave the bedroom.

"Where are we going?"

We head downstairs and along one of the many passageways. As usual, his expression is unreadable, so I have no idea where he's leading me.

Finally, he stops outside the closed doors of the grand parlor. "I know you said you were happy to forego wedding guests so we could get married right away."

"Because it was too short of notice for my friends to make it. There was no way they could get time off work and organize family in time. It would be impossible."

"Impossible for some. But not when you're married to the pakhan of the Zarkov Bratva."

"What have you done?" I ask, my excitement growing because I don't know what is on the other side of these doors. Knowing Lev, it could be anything.

"Happy wedding day, my love."

He gives me the sexiest smile I have ever seen right before he pushes the doors open.

Immediately, the room erupts with wolf cries and clapping as Chloe, Samantha, Elsa, and Henry come rushing toward us.

"When did you..? how did..?" I hug them all.

"We just got here," Henry says, pulling me in for a bear hug. "You know how I ran out of vacation time? Apparently, it was an error. HR found an extra week owed to me which is quite extraordinary considering I haven't worked there long enough to have earned it." He winks. "I think you married a wizard, baby girl."

"'Tell me about it," Samantha says with sparkling eyes. "My boss rang me before I even received the invite. Told me to take all the time I needed. Next thing I know, I'm being picked up by a limousine and taken to a private jet where these guys were waiting inside. I agree with Henry—you married a magic man. My boss hates me. She never calls.

Never gives me an iota of her time. But one call from your husband and I've got *all the time I need*."

"Does he have a brother?" Chloe asks.

"No, he has a cousin, but look away honey, I've got dibs," Henry says, watching Feliks walking in.

His arm is in a sling, but he is dressed in a fresh suit and looks good.

After many hugs are shared, and I fill my friends in on the wedding, and everyone gets a good look at my engagement and wedding ring—not to mention my growing belly—we sit at the table and enjoy our wedding feast.

The grand parlor is set up for a small reception. A long table gleams with crystalware and fine china, and the aroma of delicious food fills the air. Plates of roast chicken and beef, and dishes of roast potatoes, vegetables, gravies, and other sides crowd the table.

Across the table from me, Lev is in deep conversation with Feliks and Henry, and as I watch them, I notice the way Feliks has his arm slung across the back of Henry's chair and is tenderly stroking his shoulder as he talks. Has Cupid's arrow struck again in this house? I grin, hoping so.

Elsa leans over. "I whole-heartedly approve. Your husband is something else."

"You only just met him."

"Yes, but he clearly loves you. The man moved mountains for us all to be here today because he knew it would make you happy."

I mock gasp. "You mean he gets the Elsa tick of approval?"

"Two ticks. Because the way he looks at you... well, that man is smitten." She winks and places a gentle hand on my stomach. "And this... I couldn't be happier for you."

"I'm sorry I didn't tell you about being pregnant. Everything happened so fast. I promise I'll fill you in later."

Chloe appears beside us. "You bet you will. I want all the details." She gives me a big squeeze. "I'm so happy for you, Brooke."

"Me too," Samantha says, joining us. "I can already tell you two were made for each other."

I look over at the man I now call my husband.

My friends all love him.

But nothing like I do. Because I'm crazy in love with him.

And now everything feels right in the world.

EPILOGUE

The cry comes from very deep within me.

"It's okay, *zayka*, we'll be at the hospital in fifteen minutes," Lev tries soothing me.

But I don't have fifteen minutes.

The baby is coming.

"You need to stop the car," I cry to Feliks. "I won't make it to the hospital."

Twenty minutes ago, my water broke without warning, so Lev had Feliks drive while he sat with me in the back of the Escalade. We weren't worried to begin with. After all, I didn't get my first contraction until I climbed in the car. But ever since that very first one, they've come on hard and fast.

I let out another roar. It's like I'm being pulled apart from the inside out.

How is it that my contractions have gone from zero to a thousand in mere minutes? Isn't labor supposed to take hours? How is it that I wasn't even thinking about contractions an hour ago, but now I'm wondering if I'm going to give birth on the side of the road?

Oh my God, I'm going to give birth on the side of the road.

"Pull the fuck over," I yell in a voice I don't even recognize.

Feliks looks at Lev in the rearview mirror for guidance. "Don't look at him," I growl. "He's not the one about to squeeze a goddamn watermelon out of his vagina."

Lev squeezes my hand. "My love, we need to get you to the hospital."

"There's no time. She's coming." I reach down between my legs. "I can feel her."

Lev looks at Feliks. "Pull over and call the hospital. Tell them what's happening and where we are."

Feliks does as his cousin tells him to and immediately calls the hospital while Lev tries to make me comfortable in the back seat.

Panicked, I look up at him. "Lev, tell me I'm not about to have our baby in the back seat of this car."

He gently parts my thighs, and even though his face remains calm and unreadable, his eyes tell a different story.

"It appears so," he says calmly. "But it's going to be okay, my love. I've got this."

Another contraction racks my body, and I let out an almighty cry.

I start to pant. "Do you know what to do? Have you ever helped a woman deliver her baby?"

He gives me a charming grin. "There is a first time for everything."

I grab him as another contraction hits and grit my teeth. "Now is not the time for first times."

Oh God. This is really happening.

Feliks, who is standing outside the car, clears his throat. "As it happens, I do have experience in this area."

"What do you mean?" I snap.

"My family might be bratva, but before that, we were farmers. I grew up on a dairy farm and helped deliver more than my fair share of calves."

"I'm not a cow," I cry, tears and sweat sliding down my face.

Feliks grins. "I have experience bringing human babies into the world too. When I was sixteen, I had to deliver my neighbor's twins sons. Long story. The short version is we were in a flood and miles from medical help, and I was the only one around who could do it." He shrugs. "Sometimes you've just got to do what you've got to do."

"You're not delivering this baby," Lev says possessively.

"Why not?" I demand between gritted teeth.

"I'm thinking of your modesty, zayka. You might feel different about it later."

I'm a sweaty mess whose insides feel like they're being pulled out of her. I don't have time for his possessiveness.

I grab his collar. "I don't give a rat's ass if the entire team of the New York Rangers is down there having a look at my coochie right now. You let him get down there and help get this baby out of me."

He looks pained. I know he's trying to protect me from whatever embarrassment I might feel later. But right now I need him to back away and let Feliks do what he's got to do.

He reluctantly agrees and moves aside so his cousin can deliver this baby. He walks around to the other passenger door and slides in behind me. I lean against his powerful body and feel instantly safer. I can do this.

Crawling into the backseat, Feliks does the sign of the cross and gives the man above a nod before looking between my legs.

"I need to push," I pant.

He nods. "I can see the head, so I'm going to need you to take a deep breath and then push. Can you do that?"

I nod and suck in a deep breath, then push with all my might.

"We have the head," Feliks says with a big smile. "Next will come the shoulders, so I'm going to need you to give me another big push."

I do as he says. I push hard. And then again.

"Okay, you're doing really good, Brooke," Feliks says. "We're almost there. But I need another big push from you."

I shake my head. I'm too spent.

But Lev takes my hand and presses it to his lips. His eyes are full of love and affection and pride. "You can do this, my queen."

I nod and grit my teeth, and with a long, loud roar, I finally bring our baby into this world.

Feliks laughs and holds the baby up. "Welcome to the world, little girl."

He places her on my chest, and I am immediately in love.

Lev pulls off his shirt and wraps it around his daughter, tenderly caressing her delicate face.

Thankfully, the ambulance arrives only moments later, and the EMTs immediately get to work, checking on our beautiful daughter, and helping me.

As they're loading me into the ambulance, I turn my attention to Feliks.

"Are things going to be awkward between us?" I ask as my daughter makes adorable noises in my arms. "I mean, you got to see more of me than you probably ever thought you would."

He grins and gives me a wink. "I've already forgotten."

An hour later, sitting up in my hospital bed holding my daughter, I can still hardly believe I am a mother.

"Are you ready to hold her?" I ask Lev.

He grins and takes her from me and nestles her in his strong arms. He's still shirtless, but he's wearing his suit jacket over his naked torso. He refused to go home to get a new shirt because it would take precious time away from his newborn daughter.

"Hello, my angel," he whispers gently to her, gazing down onto her sweet face with complete affection.

"That's it, that's her name!" I say, sitting up straighter.

Since arriving at the hospital, everyone has been asking me her name.

Lev looks over at me. "You want to call her Angel?"

It seems crazy that we've never discussed names before now. Although, at the time we were caught in the middle of a mafia war. So I suppose there's that.

"It seems pretty perfect to me, don't you think?"

Lev's gaze drops to his daughter, who stirs in his arms and then settles. "Angel." He smiles, and I can see the love he already has for her in his eyes. "It's perfect."

I can't help but smile. "Angel Zarkov. It has a good ring to it."

"Angel Ivy Zarkov," Lev adds.

I feel a wash of emotion come over me. "You want to give her my mother's name?"

He nods, and I have to fight back tears.

If my mom and dad were still alive, they would play a huge role in Angel's life, and in the moment, I feel the ache of their absence right down to my core. But then I am reminded that Angel will be surrounded by a big circle of uncles and aunts, not born of blood, but still family. Uncle Feliks just helped bring her into this world, and I can't imagine that bond ever breaking. Plus, Igor and Enya, not to mention Henry and Elsa, and Samantha and Chloe. This kid is going to be spoiled with love.

I swipe away the tears. "Thank you," I whisper.

He looks from me to his daughter, and the look on his face makes me fall in love with him all over again.

I have never felt so content. So happy.

I look at them together. My perfect little family.

And I know I couldn't want for anything more.

THE END

Bonus Scene
Igor and Enya get married, and Brooke has some surprising news for Lev
https://dl.bookfunnel.com/ttvclfjmdt

More Mafia Romance by Penny Dee
De Kysa Mafia
The Devil's Den (De Kysa Mafia book 1)
The Devil's Lair (De Kysa Mafia book 2)

ALSO BY PENNY DEE

The Kings of Mayhem Original Series

Kings of Mayhem

Brothers in Arms

Biker Baby

Hell on Wheels

Off Limits

Bull

The Kings of Mayhem Tennessee Series

Jack

Doc

Ares

ABOUT THE AUTHOR

Penny Dee writes contemporary romance about rock stars, bikers, hockey players, mafia kings, and everyone in-between. Her stories bring the suspense, the feels, and a whole lot of heat.

She found her happily ever after with an Australian hottie who she met on a blind date.

Printed in Great Britain
by Amazon